ON T̶ ̶ ̶ ̶ ̶ ̶ D

"What happened?" Hanover pressed.

"We heard them arguing," Chad said. "But we couldn't see them. Then Ann shouted something."

"What?"

" 'Don't!' "

"She shouted the word *don't?*"

"Yes."

"In fear?" Hanover asked.

"Yes." Chad dropped his hands back in his lap and closed his eyes. "Then she screamed."

"Ann screamed?"

"Yes."

"What was it like?" Hanover asked. It was a cruel question. When Chad opened his eyes, they were damp.

"It was horrible," he said.

Christopher Pike

Fall Into Darkness

AN ARCHWAY PAPERBACK
Published by POCKET BOOKS
New York London Toronto Sydney Tokyo Singapore

This book is a work of fiction. Names, characters, places and incidents are products of the author's imagination or are used fictitiously. Any resemblance to actual events or locales or persons, living or dead, is entirely coincidental.

AN ARCHWAY PAPERBACK *Original*

An Archway Paperback published by
POCKET BOOKS, a division of Simon & Schuster Inc.
1230 Avenue of the Americas, New York, NY 10020

ISBN: 0-671-00984-2

First Archway Paperback printing February 1990

10 9 8 7 6 5 4 3 2 1

AN ARCHWAY PAPERBACK and colophon are registered trademarks of Simon & Schuster Inc.

Cover art by NBC Photo: Alan Zenuk

Printed in the U.S.A.

IL: 8+

For Mr. Scott

Fall Into Darkness

In the Courtroom

THE TRIAL WAS FOR MURDER. SHARON MCKAY STOOD accused. She was supposed to have killed a girl named Ann Rice. It made for wonderful headlines: the poor and talented Sharon destroying the rich and beautiful Ann in a fit of rage. Pushed Ann off the side of a cliff no less, the papers said. Nasty girl, that Sharon McKay. The media were having a field day. The two had been best friends.

But I'm innocent, Sharon McKay thought accurately enough.

No one believed her. There were three witnesses to the crime, all good kids, friends of both Ann and Sharon. And never mind that none of them had seen a thing, and that there was no body. The oddsmakers had Sharon McKay heading upriver soon. For about twenty years.

The trial was minutes from starting. Wearing her favorite blue dress and trying hard to hide her fear and exhaustion from the crowd that waited impatiently in the courtroom, Sharon sat to the left of her attorney, John Richmond—sly, smooth John, who preferred to be called Johnny. He had been appointed by the court to handle her case because she couldn't afford an attorney. Sharon glanced over at him as they waited for the judge to sweep through the majestic wooden doors on the right of the grand old wood-paneled courtroom. She tried to convince herself she trusted him to keep her out of jail, when she wasn't sure she would trust him to give her a ride home from school. They hadn't exactly hit it off at the start.

When had they first met? When had Ann died? Four weeks ago? God, it felt like ten times that long. Time moved slowly, Sharon thought, when one counted it by the path of the sun's rays on the bricks of one's cell. Yet she only had to turn her thoughts back to the morning after Ann's death, and the whole experience came rushing back as if she were on a psychedelic drug that hadn't worn off. John had caught her at her most vulnerable, and he knew it. He was clever, Sharon quickly realized, at finding people's weaknesses and exploiting them. The girls in jail spoke of him with both respect and scorn. John could manipulate a jury as well as a criminal. Time and again he got girls off who should have done hard time. Some of them said he was a genius. Yet the same girls also said that once they were on the outside John wanted to be *compensated*, and that he wasn't interested in money.

But they were just stories, possibly exaggerated.

On the morning she and John first met, Sharon had been up the whole night before, grieving for her best friend in a jail cell equipped with a stopped-up toilet and a middle-aged drunk who had splashed her—not once, but twice—with vomit. John had swept into her life like a knight in shining armor, ready to slay the dragon. Blond haired and blue eyed, with wide shoulders and an impeccably tailored sports coat, he looked as if he could have posed for Webster's definition of the word *yuppie*.

"Hi, my name's Johnny Richmond," he said, offering his hand and sitting down across from her before she had a chance to shake it properly. Their meeting room was a drab gray holding area, which Sharon found a questionable improvement over her cell. She had been allowed to go to the bathroom before being thrust into the room by a tight-lipped sergeant. The drunk's vomit had come off her pants with water from the sink, but not the smell of it. John didn't seem to mind. He flipped open his thin black briefcase and took out a legal-size yellow notepad.

"I'm Sharon," she mumbled, suffering from equal doses of shock and fatigue. Only twelve hours earlier she had been in the mountains having the time of her life.

"I know your name," he said. "McKay with a capital *K*. I'm the attorney who's been assigned to your case."

"Why?"

"Why what?"

"Why have you been assigned to me?"

"Last night you told the officer at the desk you couldn't afford an attorney. Don't you remember?"

"No. I mean, why do I have a case?"

John found that interesting. He leaned closer. He had perfectly straight white teeth. "You've been arrested for the murder of Ann Rice. Didn't they tell you that last night when they read you your rights and put the handcuffs on your wrists?"

"Yeah. I guess they did."

"You're sure about that? That they read your rights?"

"Yeah."

"Then that's why I'm here. To make sure you get every one of those rights guaranteed to you under the Constitution." He turned to the center of his notepad and smoothed back the pages. "You're a lucky girl. Most people in your situation would sit in jail several days before having a chance to talk to me."

She didn't feel so lucky. She disliked him already. "Really."

"I figure this is going to be a big case."

"And that's why you hurried here?"

"I take my job seriously." He pressed open the point on his pen. "Tell me what happened."

"I didn't kill Ann," she said.

He smiled. "I'm your attorney. You can tell me the truth. I won't tell anybody. I promise."

"I didn't kill her. She was my best friend. I wouldn't have hurt her for anything. She jumped off the cliff."

"Was your friend suicidal?"

"No."

"Then why did she kill herself?"

"I don't know."

"We can't tell the judge that."

"Why not? It's the truth."

"He won't believe you."

"Do you believe me?" she asked.

"I'm your attorney. I have to believe you."

He was playing with her, she knew, and on top of everything else she had gone through, it was enough to make her cry. But it wasn't her style to cry in front of anyone. It hadn't been Ann's, either.

"What if I don't want you for my attorney?" she asked.

"You can request that someone else be assigned to your case. But I wouldn't do that if I were you."

"Why not?"

He leaned forward again, closer this time, catching her eye. "Because I'm good, Sharon McKay. I'm very good. In fact, I'm the best you'll find in this state."

He was sure of himself, if nothing else. She nodded. "Very well, Mr. Richmond."

"Johnny, please."

"Johnny." She spread her hands. "What else can I tell you? I didn't push her off the cliff."

He sat back in his chair and clicked the point of his pen in and out. He couldn't have been thirty yet. From his brisk, cocky manner she figured he was a graduate of some big Ivy League school. She couldn't imagine what he was doing in Utah, except maybe trying to land an important murder case so he could run for an important office at an important future date.

"Can I be perfectly blunt with you?" he asked.

"I thought you were already being blunt."

"Have you ever been in jail before?"

"No."

"It's no fun."

"Really?" She was being sarcastic now.

"Did you get any sleep last night?" he asked.

"No. I'm exhausted. When can you get me out on bail?"

"I don't know if I can."

"What?" She had assumed bail would be a formality. All the bad guys in the movies always got out on bail. And she wasn't even guilty.

"I've already spoken to the district attorney about you," he said.

"At nine in the morning? What did he say?"

"She. Her name's Margaret Hanover. She knows as well as I that this case could turn into a media circus. She wants to make herself look tough on crime. She's working on the judge to set your bail at two hundred thousand. I think she's going to succeed. Unless your parents own plenty of property, you'd have to come up with a fair chunk of that to get out."

"My parents are divorced. My mom works in a grocery store. We don't own our own backyard." Sharon lowered her head. "Does this mean I have to go back to that cell?"

"They might transfer you to another one."

"Oh, swell."

"I'm sorry."

The note of sympathy in his voice sounded genuine. She looked up again. "I didn't push her," she repeated.

He was watching her closely. "I believe you."

"Do you tell all your clients that?"

"Not all of them. If you didn't push her, your only defense is that she killed herself."

"What if it was an accident?"

"Do you think it was an accident?"

She hesitated, knowing she might be contradicting herself. "Yes."

"The district attorney already has three witnesses that say Ann argued with you before she went over the cliff. One of them is your boyfriend."

"Fred's not my boyfriend," Sharon said.

"What is he?"

"Just a friend."

"Did Ann argue with you?"

"No."

"Why do the others say she did?"

"Because they heard Ann shouting at me."

"Was Ann in the habit of shouting at you?"

"No."

"Then I think you can see why saying it was an accident won't cut it."

Sharon nodded slowly, biting her lip. "Have they found her body yet?"

"No. But they will."

She closed her eyes. "She was so beautiful."

"That's what they tell me. You were close?"

She sniffed. "Yes."

"Can you think of any reason, any reason at all, why she might have wanted to kill herself?"

"No. But—"

"Yes?"

"Her brother committed suicide last year."

John made a note on his pad. "That's interesting. What was his name?"

"Jerry. Jerry Rice. He was a year younger than Ann and me."

"Did you know him well?"

"Yes. We dated a few times." She added hastily, "But it was just for fun."

"He wasn't your boyfriend?"

"No."

"Do you have a boyfriend?"

"No."

"Why not? You're cute."

"I don't have time for a boyfriend."

"Why not?"

"I play the piano. It takes all my time."

He nodded. "I remember now, I read about you in the paper."

"Really? What paper?"

"The *Times*. You won a scholarship to Juilliard, didn't you?"

"Yes."

"You must be good."

"I like to think so."

"I always wanted to be a musician. Had no talent for it, I'm sad to say. Did Jerry like music?"

She shrugged. "I suppose."

"Did he like to listen to you play?"

"Yeah."

"Did he like you?"

"Why do you ask?"

"Because I'm nosy. Did he?"

"Yeah."

"Did he love you?"

"No. I don't think so."

John leaned back in his chair. "Why did Jerry kill himself, Sharon?"

She stared at him. They had talked for only a few minutes, and he was asking that kind of question already. She felt like screaming at him to mind his own business; and yet right then was when she decided to have him defend her. Maybe he was the best. He had a way of pressing hidden nerves.

"I don't know," she said honestly.

A week went by. She was given another cell. She had a twenty-year-old junkie for a roommate. Her name was Mary, and when she wasn't unconscious, she was having wide-awake dreams. John visited every couple of days. They couldn't find Ann's body, he said. Sharon thought that was important, but John said no. There was no question that Ann had to be dead, he told her. She had to be. She had fallen five hundred feet off the side of a cliff into a raging river that emptied into a lake a few miles farther along. Her body could easily have disappeared into it. Sharon had to go along with this reasoning. It seemed logical.

A hearing followed. John tried to get the case thrown out. At the hearing she was guilty until proven innocent. It was the reverse of a trial, John said. But he struck out. He wasn't disappointed. He had seen it coming. But Sharon was disappointed. She was the one who had to go back to her jail cell. It was no place for a good girl. Her roommate had already found a connection on the inside and was talking to God after each fix. Sharon felt she was going insane. She hardly ever got to see her mom. And they wouldn't let her play a piano! Without her music she felt trapped. She had been foolish enough to think that writing a polite letter to the warden would get her access to an instrument. The girls in her block said the warden couldn't even read.

John pushed for a speedy trial, and because there was no huge backlog of cases, they got one. Four weeks after her arrest she sat waiting with John for the judge to appear.

But still, no body. And still, John said, it wasn't supposed to matter.

"How do you feel?" John asked, noticing her looking at him.

"OK. How about you?"

"Great. Slept like a baby last night."

"I'm glad."

"Hey, you only have to sit here and watch. I've got to do all the work." He glanced at his watch. "Where is that bastard?"

"What's Judge Warner like? Besides being a bastard?"

"He used to be one of the finest judges in the state until he had a mild stroke a couple of years back. Now he's slow. He presided over a case of mine last year and fell asleep in the middle of the prosecutor's closing remarks. But he likes me."

"Why?"

"I keep him awake."

Sharon glanced over at the prosecutor—Ms. District Attorney herself—Margaret Hanover. Sharon decided she should be flattered that the woman hadn't handed the job over to a flunky. John had already explained why she hadn't. Margaret Hanover *didn't* like John. He said it was because he had kicked her ass in court a few years back—the girls in jail said it was because he had tried to pinch her ass. Sharon couldn't imagine it. The woman was in her fifties and had one of those rare faces that had probably never looked youthful. The sharp lines around her eyes looked as if they had been cut in. Even though she wasn't the least bit overweight, she had a significant double chin. All in all she was about as ugly as they came. Sharon felt kind of sorry for her, but knew she'd feel sorrier for herself if the woman put her away.

"I spoke to your mom this morning," John said.

"How's she doing?" Sharon asked. Half the ordeal of her imprisonment had been knowing how her mother must be suffering. Her mom was very involved with the church, and how those church ladies loved to gossip behind people's backs. Whenever her mom did visit, however, she tried to sound upbeat for Sharon's sake. Sharon glanced over her shoulder, trying to pick her out in the crowd.

"She's fine," John said. "I told her we're going to win."

"And if we don't?"

"I'll win my next case." He smiled and patted her leg under the table. "That's a joke, Sharon."

"Oh."

"You've got to learn to lighten up."

She used to tell Ann that. Sharon was always the carefree one—in another lifetime. Had Ann left the brooding portion of her personality behind for Sharon to gnaw upon? Ann knew what she was doing, killing herself the way she had. It had been no accident— Sharon had figured that out by her second week in jail. Ann must have known exactly where her act would land her best friend.

But why?

There was no simple answer. No hard one. Nothing.

"I can't lighten up," she said.

"Why not? I honestly do think we'll win."

"Even if we do, my friend is still dead."

John waved his hand. "She was nuts."

Sharon grabbed his hand and pressed it down on the hard wooden table. Ann might have hated her, but she couldn't bring herself to hate Ann in return. "You can tell that to the jury if you have to," she said softly. "But don't ever say that to me. It's not true."

He met her stare. He was no one to intimidate. "Whatever."

The Honorable Franklin Warner finally entered the courtoom. Everyone stood. He was not the same judge who had presided over the selection of her jury. He had been sick that day, although today he looked fine, if a bit tired. He was a medium-size man with an oversize belly. Gray hair sprouted thick and curly from the sides of his round head, but was completely missing from his shiny top. His robe was black, of course, and it reminded Sharon of the funeral the outside world had not been able to hold for Ann because there had been nothing to bury.

The jury watched the judge's entrance with respect. Sharon found herself looking over at them in silent panic. John had told her to look at them occasionally. "Let them see your eyes and know you're a real person," he said. But they didn't look real to her. They had twelve heads but only one mouth that could speak only two phrases: "Guilty" or "Not guilty." They sat to the judge's left, Sharon's right.

The judge took his seat. The rest of the court followed. The trial was given an official name: the People versus Sharon McKay in the matter of the death of Ann Rice. The prosecutor stood to give her opening remarks. She had on a gray suit and not a speck of makeup. She turned and approached the jury impatiently.

John had told Sharon that Hanover was a master of the fine point, but a total failure when it came to understanding the fears of a juror. It was John's belief that most jurors were not so terrified of rendering a wrong verdict as they were of annoying their fellow jurors by not going along with what the group wanted. He, therefore, tried to reinforce this basic fear by making them feel that they were one big family. He further exploited it by leading them to feel that the family could only survive the trauma of the trial by doing what was *safe*, which inevitably meant the release of his client.

"Sharon McKay is eighteen years old," the D.A. began, halting at the end of the jury box closer to the judge and court reporter. Hanover fixed the collection of everyday citizens with her severe brown eyes. "She is legally an adult and is to be tried as an adult. Her young and innocent appearance and her outstanding artistic accomplishments are of no importance. Sharon McKay is a murderer, a murderer of the worst kind. For she killed a friend, someone who trusted her with her life."

Hanover paused and stared directly at Sharon, raising her voice, addressing not only the jury but the entire courtroom. "The people will show that on the night of June sixteenth, approximately one month ago, Sharon McKay did willfully push Ann Rice off the side of a cliff, five hundred feet to her death. The people will further show that this was a premeditated act, and that it should carry with it the verdict of murder in the first degree. The people will call several witnesses to this abominable act, and will leave not a trace of a doubt that Sharon McKay has committed murder."

Sharon felt mortally wounded. She couldn't have killed anyone to save her life. She felt as if she were sinking deeper into her seat, even though she knew she was sitting perfectly rigid with her breath held. John leaned over and whispered in her ear.

"Relax, babe. Hanover's just trying to spice up her act. She's already lost half the jury with her fancy rhetoric."

Sharon swallowed and nodded weakly. But she felt ashamed to look at the jury for what she hadn't even done. She was also ashamed of herself for being so easily flustered. Hanover glared at her as she strode back to her seat.

It was John's turn. He jumped up eagerly, as if he were the top student in his math class and had just been called on to work out a simple problem on the board. He didn't stride directly toward the jury, but strolled casually to the far end of the rail that separated them from the spectators. There he rested one hand lightly on the smooth wooden rail, raising his other hand to his well-defined jaw, keeping his head down, thinking, so it seemed, of the many options from which he could choose to respond to Hanover's ridiculous accusations. He stood that way for several moments without saying a word. The entire court was focused on him. Then he suddenly clapped his hands together, and everyone jumped.

"Sharon didn't kill Ann," he said. "Why would she kill her? They were buddies. The whole idea is preposterous. There is no motive. There are no witnesses. This thing should never have come to trial. But this is an election year, and we have to put up with dramatics like this." John paused and smiled reassuringly. "Well, I'm not concerned for Sharon. I've found the truth has a habit of shining through the lies. Don't worry, folks. Your decision will be a simple one."

That was all John said. He returned to his seat and sat down. Sharon was impressed. The members of the jury were exchanging glances as if they were members of a group, rather than staring forward as isolated individuals. They already liked John. Maybe they would like her, too.

The prosecution began by calling Chad Lear to the stand.

Chad was a big question mark for Sharon. While preparing for the trial, John had asked her if Chad would go against her. She had responded by saying that Chad would tell the truth. Yet she knew what John meant. There was the truth and there was the truth. Chad was an old friend of Sharon's, but an even older friend of Ann's. He could even have been in love with Ann—Sharon wasn't sure. The sight of him as he walked to the stand made her wonder all the more. Ann's death had obviously devastated him. Chad had always been thin, but now he was a bag of bones. His curly brown hair hung long and uncombed over the sides of his head. The loss of weight made his prominent nose and large moist eyes appear to jump out of his face. His head was down as he was sworn in, and he only looked up when Hanover walked up for her first question. But when Chad did raise his head it was in Sharon's direction. He smiled faintly, a sad smile.

"What was your relationship to Ann Rice?" Hanover began.

"I was a close friend of hers and her brother's," Chad responded, his soft voice softer than usual. "I was also an employee of hers. I took care of her place, did the gardening and stuff."

"How old are you, Chad?"

"Seventeen."

"You're a year younger than Ann?"

"Yes."

"And a year younger than the defendant? Sharon McKay?"

"Yes."

"How long had you known Ann?" Hanover asked.

"Since we were little. I don't know—ten years, maybe."

"It would be reasonable to say you knew her well?"

"Yes," Chad said.

"Tell us about Ann's house? She was well-off, wasn't she?"

"Yes. She was worth several million. She had a great place. It was a mansion. It still is. The grounds cover over twelve acres. They keep me busy."

"Did she like her house?"

"Sure," Chad said.

"Tell us how Ann Rice came to be so rich?"

"She inherited the money from her mother."

"Who died of a heart attack last year?"

"They think it was a heart attack."

Hanover took a step closer to Chad. She hadn't wanted him to raise a question about the cause of Mrs. Rice's death. Chad clasped his hands together in his lap and glanced uneasily at the jury. Sharon could practically feel the sweat gathering between his palms. It couldn't be easy for him to speak of Ann in front of all these strangers.

"Whose idea was it to go on the camping trip?" Hanover asked.

"Mine, I suppose. We all talked about it. I knew the area the best. Ann was excited about going."

John made a note on his pad.

"Excited?" Hanover asked.

"Yes," Chad said.

"She was on the verge of graduating from high school. Was she excited about that?"

"She was looking forward to getting out."

"What were her plans for the future?"

"I don't know," Chad said.

Hanover had not expected that answer. Sharon had no trouble reading the woman's body language. John would have called it another one of Hanover's weaknesses as a prosecutor. Hanover had just indirectly told the jury she had previously gone over these questions with Chad.

"But she did have plans for her life, didn't she?" Hanover asked. "Hadn't she just gotten engaged?"

Chad smiled briefly. "Yeah. To my brother."

"Did she love your brother?"

"Oh, sure."

"He made her happy?" Hanover asked.

"Yes."

"Her life was just beginning. She had money. She had love. Didn't she, in fact, have what most people want out of life?"

Chad hesitated. "I suppose."

Hanover shifted to Chad's left, placing him between

her and the jury, giving them a clear, unobstructed view of his response. "Chad," she said, "in your opinion, knowing Ann for as long as you did, would you say she was suicidal?"

"No," Chad replied.

Did I expect him to say yes when I would have had to say no? Sharon asked herself.

The answer was no. Yet Sharon suddenly felt as if the trial could run away from her before John had a chance to defend her. She leaned close to John, whispering in his ear, "Why don't you object or something?"

"You're sure about this?" Hanover asked.

"Objection," John said. "The witness is being called upon to give an answer to a question that even a psychiatrist would hesitate to answer with absolute certainty."

"Sustained," Judge Warner said.

"Thanks," Sharon muttered.

"Don't thank me," John whispered back. "Winning objections does not translate into winning jurors. You've been watching too much TV. Listen closely. Chad isn't against us."

"I don't know about that," Sharon said.

"I do," John replied confidently.

"Tell the court what happened the night of June sixteenth?" Hanover asked.

"We camped at the top of Westwind. That's a peak in Sunset National Park. It's not too high, maybe three thousand feet. It's a good place to camp because it has a view of the whole park, and shelter, too. I know that area well. I've hiked there since I was a kid."

"Go on," Hanover said.

"A bunch of us were sitting at the campfire. We were singing songs, eating, drinking, having a good time. Then Sharon and Ann decided to go for a walk."

"Whose idea was it to go for the walk?"

Chad paused, looking uneasy. "I think it was Sharon's. They picked up a flashlight and headed away from the fire in the direction of a cliff. We had gotten there before dark, so both of them had an idea of the layout of the area. The cliff jutted out a few feet from the side directly above Whipping River." Chad lowered his head again as if he were looking down into the river. "This time of year it's full from melting snow. It was running hard."

"Could either of the girls have first headed for the cliff and then circled around behind you without the three of you knowing it?"

"I doubt it," Chad said.

"There was only one path to the cliff?"

"Yes."

"Please continue."

Chad's right cheek twitched. Taking a deep breath and shifting in his seat, he pressed the tips of his unsteady fingers to his chin. "They walked away from the campfire, like I said. They were only gone for a few minutes. I watched them go. I told them to be careful. I knew the place better than any of them. I should have gone with them."

"What happened?" Hanover pressed.

"We heard them arguing," Chad said. "But we couldn't see them. Then Ann shouted something."

"What?"

" 'Don't.' "

"She shouted the word *don't?*"

19

"Yes."

"Loud?"

"Yes."

"In fear?" Hanover asked.

"Yes." Chad dropped his hands back in his lap and closed his eyes. "Then she screamed."

"Ann screamed?"

"Yes."

"She screamed as she fell to her death?"

"Yes."

"What was it like?" Hanover asked. It was a cruel question. When Chad opened his eyes, they were damp.

"It was horrible," he said.

CHAPTER ONE

Ann Rice's hate was alive. It fed her and gave her strength. It gave her purpose. Sometimes she actually felt it was her life. But she hated it—the hating. She had not asked for it. She had never asked for anything, never had to. Everything had always been handed to her: fancy cars, beautiful clothes, pretty boys. Her pretty face had always gotten her plenty of boys. But nothing could give her what she wanted now—her brother brought back to life. Her fat bank balance certainly couldn't. And her hate could at best only bring her another death.

But if I ruin Sharon, what will become of what I've become?

Ann often wondered that. Would her hate suddenly cease and leave her in peace? Or would it just find another outlet? She honestly didn't know, but she was smart enough to realize that perhaps none of it would make any difference in the way she felt. At eighteen, Ann was already a keen student of human nature. She knew what small rewards and heavy penalties usually came to those who sought revenge. But because she was smart she thought she would be the exception. Her planning was meticulous. Nothing had been left to chance.

Except Paul, my darling Paul.

At present Ann was waiting for Paul Lear. She was standing on top of the hill that overlooked her school —Wonderwood High, one of Utah's best, a quaint collection of aged brick buildings nestled together like a happy family at the end of a valley that had years before been stripped of the last of its wonderful woods. She had attended classes that morning, but since she was a senior and had completed her graduation requirements she usually wandered far from campus in the afternoons. She had returned to meet Paul and go over her plan for Sharon. She also wanted to see Sharon. Paul knew what she wanted to discuss because when she had said good night to him the previous night, she had given him a hint.

"I can't take it anymore, Paul. She has to go."

Then she had kissed him on the lips and scooted him out the door before he could reply so that she could at least get a couple hours of sleep before the sun came up. But she hadn't slept. She had lain awake in her black and closed-up room trying to visualize what it would be like to fall and never hit the ground.

It was a hot day. Ann loved the heat. She was a person of extremes. She loved to lie sweating in the sun by the swimming pool, straight on the concrete deck without a towel beneath her, and let her skin fry a golden brown. Paul thought she was crazy, and maybe she was. She was crazy about him. She loved him almost as much as she hated Sharon.

Almost. Such a word—two neat syllables with which to sharpen one's regret. Jerry had almost lived. Had the barrel of the gun been a centimeter to the right, or an inch to the left, he might have been standing beside her now, waiting, as she was, to see his beloved Sharon. God, how Jerry had loved Sharon. Of course, that was the trouble with bullets. They didn't understand centimeters or inches. But Ann understood why Jerry had pulled the trigger. He had also been a person of extremes. It ran in the family. No wonder both their parents had died of heart attacks before the age of sixty. Too much stress. Too many almosts.

Just then Paul drove up and parked at the base of the hill, in the lot at the back of the school. He waved to her as he climbed out. He needed a new car. He had to borrow his brother's to get around. She had tried to buy him one a couple of weeks earlier, but he said no. He had accepted the clothes she bought for him, though. He was wearing the black slacks and black silk shirt she had picked out. Black suited his dark gypsy features. It suited the smoldering look in his deep brown eyes. It was his eyes that had first attracted her to him. He was a couple of years older than she was and had already spent a year in the navy. It seemed when she looked into his eyes that she could see a gray storm approaching over a turbulent sea. But only if she looked deep. On the outside, he was calm. He hadn't had a steady job since he had gotten out of the navy and was a bit of a drifter. But he had energy to burn for those things he had a passion for—and she was one of them. They often stayed up half the night, burning both ends of a candle that threatened to explode. They had their share of fights.

Paul was rough material, and basically they had little in common. He didn't read. He had no interest in world affairs. He probably knew less than a tenth of what she knew. Yet he had a hold over her. Like a book that tantalized with each turned page, he had a body she couldn't put down. His mind was also fascinating, what she had seen of it. She didn't understand him and never knew where he was coming from, and that made him a mystery she wanted to solve. Perhaps that was the one thing they *did* have in common—for she didn't really understand herself, either. She didn't think anybody did, or could.

She raised her arm and waved back. "I said two-thirty," she called.

He checked his watch as he came up the hill, the sweat on his forehead glistening in the rays of the hot sun. It was not the short hike up the hill, however, that was causing him to perspire. He was in excellent shape. He worked out regularly with weights. He was a hunk; he could pick her up with one hand, and lay her down with the pressure of his baby finger.

"I was helping Chad finish the wall," he said. His brother was repairing a stone wall on the north corner of her property. Chad cared more about the place than she did.

"Then you'll have to let me pay you," she said.

He nodded. "Two grand should cover it."

"I'll write you a check," she said, offering him her arms. He pulled her toward him and gave her a brief hard kiss that momentarily flattened her full lips. Paul had never really learned to kiss, not the way a woman typically wants to be kissed, and for that she was glad. She wasn't a typical woman.

"What am I doing here?" he asked the moment they parted.

She brushed a thick strand of hair from his forehead. They had the same color hair, a brown so dark it was really black. But whereas hers was soft as a summer breeze, his was thick, like a weave of strong string.

Or rope. I could hang myself with that rope.

But that was not true. She could die, but she would not hang.

She smiled. "You're here to see me."

"What were you talking about last night?"

"Aren't you going to ask me about my day first?"

"How was your day?" he asked impatiently.

She started to laugh, but stopped short. "Don't you know what day it is?" she asked softly.

"No."

"It was a year ago today."

He hesitated. "No, it wasn't. Jerry died in August."

She turned away, back toward the school. "I didn't mean that. Today was his birthday. It *is* his birthday. A year ago today he was sixteen."

"I'm sorry."

"Paul? Why are so many songs written about people who are sixteen? Do you think it's because it's the transition between youth and adulthood?"

"It's probably because the word *sixteen* rhymes with a lot of other words." He put his hand on her shoulder. "Ann, you've got to stop thinking about it. It's done with."

She continued to stare down at the school. She had gone to it for four years, and—it was weird—she hardly recognized it. "I don't want to let it go," she whispered.

"You should stop seeing her, then."

"I don't want to stop seeing her."

"What do you want?" he asked.

"Did you know I've taken up skydiving?"

"So you're trying to kill yourself, is that it?"

"They say it's statistically safer than driving the freeways."

"I don't believe that," he said.

"It's as safe as rock climbing. Chad's been teaching me that at Sunset National Park. Did you know that?"

"No. When have you been doing all this?"

She turned back to him, and his hand fell from her shoulder. "Here and there. Rock climbing and sky diving have a lot in common. In one you're daring yourself to fall, and in the other you just fall."

"Talk some sense or I'm leaving."

She nodded. "You're right. I need to let it go. I need to get away from all this nothingness." She gestured to the school beneath them, to the whole valley. "I hate this place."

"Then let's go to Mexico this summer."

"We can go to Mexico. . . ." she said, letting the sentence hang.

He was on his guard. For all he loved her—and she

knew he loved her as much as she did him—he didn't trust her a hundred percent. That was fine. She wouldn't have trusted herself a hundred percent, either.

"We can go after we do what?" he asked, reading her mind. "I'm not going to hurt her."

"Hurt her? I don't want to *hurt* her. Did she just *hurt* Jerry?"

"She didn't do anything to Jerry."

She was suddenly angry. "That's right! She didn't do a thing! She let him fall in love with her, and then she just let him be. She didn't have time to do anything to him. She doesn't have time for anybody."

"She makes time for you."

She smiled bitterly. "I know."

"Let it go, Ann. You're driving yourself crazy."

"I can't."

"Why can't you?"

"I can't! Don't you see that about me?" The question ached to be asked. Yet she wished she had left it unspoken. It was not in her nature to show weakness. That had been one of the worst things about losing her brother. It had put a portion of her soul on display for one miserable day that had lasted an eternity. She had cried at his funeral in front of everybody. She hadn't cried since, nor had she any intention of doing so again.

"What are you going to do?" Paul asked.

"Destroy her."

"How?"

"I'm going to need your help, Paul."

"You'll end up in jail."

"Impossible," she said.

"Is that why you've planned this trip to the park? Are you going to push her off a cliff?"

"It can be done without laying a hand on her."

"Tell me, damnit," he snapped.

She spoke methodically. "There's a peak in Sunset Park called Westwind. A cliff juts out from it above Whipping River. The first night of our trip we're going to camp there, and when we're all settled around the fire, Sharon and I are going to go for a little walk—to the edge of the cliff. We'll look at the stars, maybe talk about old times, and then I'm going to tell Sharon I'd like to be alone for a few minutes. Sharon'll head back for the fire, and when she's halfway there, I'm going to reach behind a nearby boulder and attach a rope to a clip hidden under my sweatshirt. I'm going to shout the word *don't* as loud as I can, and then I'm going to jump off the cliff and scream my bloody heart out."

"You're crazy."

"It won't be an ordinary rope that's clipped to my back. The fall from the tip of the cliff to the surface of the water is exactly five hundred and ten feet. My rope is four hundred and ten feet long. It will be attached fifty feet below the edge of the cliff. The last fifteen feet of my rope is elastic. It will stretch. Taking into account the length of my fall and my body weight, the rope should stretch an additional ten feet at the end of my fall. When I am through bouncing, I'll attach a second rope to the end of the first rope and clip it under my sweatshirt also. Then I'll unsnap the first rope. This second rope is exactly fifty feet long. It'll be longer than I need to lower myself to the side of the river. Then I will disappear, and everybody will think Sharon pushed me to my death."

"Hardly. What about the rope hanging from the side of the cliff? Everyone will see it."

"No one will see it. It will be a moonless night, I checked. And I told you, the rope isn't attached to the top of the cliff, but to a point fifty feet over the side. I attached it there myself three days ago with a metal pin. That's where I need you. I need you to go over the side of the cliff and release that rope. You'll let it fall down to me, and I'll take it with me when I leave."

"To where?"

"Anywhere. Mexico—it doesn't matter. I'll just disappear." She took a step toward him, placed her palm on the muscled curve of his chest, and stared him straight in the eye. "You can go with me."

He shook his head. "This will never work."

She took a step back, not annoyed. She had expected a round of objections. "Tell me why it won't work, and I'll tell why it will."

"There are a thousand reasons why."

"List them," she said.

"First, if you fall that far, the rope will wrench you in two."

"I told you, the end will stretch. Rock climbers use this kind of equipment all the time."

"Rock climbers don't use it to jump five hundred feet."

"I'll wear a harness under my sweatshirt to help break my fall."

"It won't help if you smack the wall of the cliff."

"The top of the cliff juts way out from the cliff wall.

The chances of my hitting the wall are one in a hundred."

"Fifty-fifty is probably more like it. What if we don't camp there? What if Chad wants to camp somewhere else?"

"Chad always camps there when he goes rock climbing. It's one of his favorite spots."

"What if there are other campers around?"

"Then we'll wait and do it another time."

He shook his head again. "When you go off the cliff, everybody will run over to see what's happened. They'll see you dangling there."

"I told you, there'll be no moon. You can't see a thing at night in the mountains when there's no moon. It'll be pitch-black."

"What excuse can I use to go over the cliff to release the metal pin?"

"It'll be a normal panic reaction for someone to go over the cliff. Tell them it'll take forty minutes to hike to the bottom. There might be a chance I landed on a ledge, you can say. And then, when you climb down, if they follow you with their flashlights, tell them to turn the lights away, that they're blinding you. But this is very important. Don't undo the rope till you make sure I'm down."

"But I won't be able to see you," Paul protested.

"You don't have to. Just make sure the tension has gone out of the rope. Anyway, I should be on the ground well before you're ready to pull out the pin."

"If the pin's in deep enough to withstand your fall, I won't be able to get it out without a crowbar."

"It is in deep," Ann admitted. "It will be better if you can get it out. Perhaps you could have a long screwdriver with you, hidden under your jacket. But if you don't get it out, don't panic. Just undo the rope. No one's going to look for a pin fifty feet down the side of the cliff."

"Can I ask you something?"

"Certainly."

"Why are you doing this?" Paul asked.

"To destroy Sharon."

"That's insane. No one will believe she pushed you off the cliff. Everybody thinks you're best friends."

"What else can they think? That I committed suicide?"

"When your body doesn't show up, they'll think you set this whole thing up and that you are down in Mexico drinking margaritas."

"Chad told me about three bridge builders who fell to their deaths a couple years ago in Whipping River. Two of the bodies were never found. They disappeared into Winter Lake. I can disappear into that lake, too."

"It won't work, Ann."

"You keep saying that! Why not?"

"You want Sharon held responsible for your death. Don't you read the newspapers? Prosecutors have trouble convicting murderers when they've been caught with a bloody knife in their hands and somebody's head in their car trunk. Face it, you need a body."

Ann nodded. "I know it's difficult to be convicted of *first*-degree murder when there's no body. But there's an excellent chance Sharon will be convicted of a lesser crime. But even that's not necessary. Look at her life. She has everything in order. She has her music. She has her scholarship to Juilliard. Everybody likes and respects her. She has friends. But do you think Juilliard is going to want a girl who's stood trial for murder? Do you think people everywhere aren't going to wonder, for the rest of her life, if she actually did it? And don't you think Sharon will at least figure out the half of it, that I did this to her on purpose, that I killed myself because I hated her? That will eat at her more than anything precisely because I am her best friend." Ann forced a chuckle. "I don't need a conviction. Her life will be in ruins."

"Say all this works and there is a trial," Paul said. "I'll be called to the stand. What am I supposed to say?"

"What the others say. That's all you should know."

"But what if Sharon is convicted and then I suddenly disappear? It'll look suspicious."

"How? You weren't even close to me when I went over the cliff. How can you be held even remotely responsible? You're looking at this backward. This *is* a bizarre plan. No one will even consider it a possibility."

"I wonder. How did you think of it?"

Ann paused. "I don't know. Where does any idea come from? But there was a book I read not too long ago that might have inspired me. It was about a girl who wanted to get back at her friends by setting them up for her murder."

"I still don't like how all this will look for me."

"Are you worried because I've put you in my will?" Paul took a step back. "Now that's dumb."

"Wherever we end up, we'll need money. I've already moved cash south of the border into a safe-deposit box, but we'll need more." She smiled. "I thought you'd be pleased to inherit a small fortune."

"Where are you going to go once you're down?" Paul asked.

"I bought a getaway car. I'll have it parked somewhere close to the river. I haven't decided exactly where yet."

"Someone might trace the car back to you."

"Impossible. It's hot."

Paul paused. "Something just occurred to me, Ann."

"What?"

"I can't believe we're even discussing this."

"Why not?" she asked sharply. "You know how I feel about her."

"What about how I feel? I have no grudge against Sharon. Why should I help you?"

"Because you love me."

He thought about that for a moment and then looked away. "How much is that small fortune?"

She hit him. "Is that all I am to you?"

He grabbed her hands and spoke seriously. "No. I don't care about your money. I care about you. It could take months for this to blow over. During that time, I won't even be able to see you. It'll be dangerous to talk to you on the phone."

She had thought of that, but decided it would be worth it. Just barely. She really did need him, and not just to undo the rope.

She remembered the first time they met, a little over a year before. Paul hadn't gone to school with them. He had grown up on the West Coast. Chad had introduced them. Chad and Paul were only half brothers, sharing the same father. They didn't look a bit alike. When Chad had told her his brother was stopping by the house, she expected another skinny runt. What a pleasant surprise the meeting turned out to be. The instant she saw Paul, something passed between them. Of course, Paul later denied it was true, but even Chad said he felt it.

Paul's mother was first-generation Italian, and he had inherited her dark olive skin and thick sensual lips. When he smiled, he looked remarkably friendly, but when he was in a bad mood, he appeared nothing short of dangerous—he had that kind of mouth.

Paul had only been out of the navy a couple of months when they met. Back then he had been like a savage let loose after being cooped up for months on a ship. He hadn't gotten along with many of his shipmates, but she wasn't sure why. He didn't like talking about the past.

"If we plan it right, we should be able to exchange a few phone calls," she said in response to his remark.

"What are you going to do about Chad?" Paul asked.

"We can't tell him," she said.

"That doesn't answer my question. It would kill him if he thought you were dead. You saw what losing Jerry did to him."

Ann sighed. Chad was one of the few who had cared. "He still blames himself—to this day."

"What are you going to tell him?"

She lowered her head. This would be almost as bad as losing Paul for several months. "Nothing," she whispered.

"Ann."

She looked up. "I can't answer that. You know that. But I've answered all your other objections. It's going to work, Paul. Will you help me?"

Down the hill, the bell rang. Paul turned to watch the students pour out of classes. He was thinking, and she didn't press him for an answer because she already knew what it would be. When he had gotten out of the navy, he cussed a lot, but he stopped when she had asked him to. She was asking for more this time. But if someone loved you, she thought, it was all relative. He'd say yes, she knew it.

But before he could respond, Sharon and Chad spotted them on top of the hill. They waved and Ann waved back. Watching them start on the short hike up the hill, Ann felt disgusted that anyone as smart as Sharon should be such a fool when it came to understanding her closest friend. Yet there was much to admire about Sharon, she knew. They hadn't become friends by accident. They met during their freshman year. Even back then Sharon had been an extraordinary musician. Ann heard her music before she saw her face. She had a first-period art class with a desk next to a wall that adjoined the music wing, and every morning, through that wall, she would hear the finest composers of the past being played with a passion and sensitivity that impressed Ann. It was hard for someone as proud as Ann to admit it, but she was in awe of Sharon. It was she who sought Sharon out. She felt that for Sharon to play as beautifully as she did, she must be a beautiful person. But later, when Jerry was dead, Ann wondered if Sharon ever felt the depth of emotion of any of her pieces, if Sharon wasn't simply a clinical technician who could play a sonata as flawlessly as an executive secretary might type an error-free letter.

Sharon had other qualities that drew Ann to her. Sharon was sweet. People liked her, and for Ann, who'd had few friends before the ninth grade, watching Sharon move easily through a crowd at lunchtime filled her with both envy and affection, the former because she knew she'd never be as popular as Sharon, the latter because she was also a victim of Sharon's charms. But it was what they had in common that made them close. Sharon gave the impression of giving freely of herself to others, but it was only for short periods of time, and never fully or completely. Sharon always held back a part that she never showed to anybody. Ann recognized it and understood it because she also held back a part of herself. This understanding of the other went unspoken between them, but it also bound them together, allowing them to be equals.

Still, it came as a shock to Ann that Sharon would one day play her brother for a sucker.

Sharon always flirted with Ann's younger brother, Jerry. Even when Jerry was only in eighth grade and not interested in girls yet, Sharon would smile her lovely smile and compliment him on a painting he had done, even though it was obvious to Ann that Sharon actually thought Jerry would be better off spending his time painting the walls of the house. But Ann had permitted the flirting, not understanding that as Jerry grew into a young man, his affection would naturally flow toward the one girl who had always encouraged him. Even when Jerry asked Sharon out, Ann hadn't understood the depth of his feeling for Sharon. She had only guessed at it in the months after their first date, when he would act moody on the days Sharon failed to return his calls.

It wasn't until Ann came home late one night the previous August and found Jerry curled up on his bed with a gun in his mouth and specks of skull and brain on his pillow that she really understood, not just her brother and his feelings, but Sharon as well. In that moment, horrible as it had been, Ann experienced a clarity of thought that was to stay with her to this day, a clarity that had allowed her to think the unthinkable. Sharon was a bad person and therefore she had to be destroyed. It was very simple. And then, months later, Ann's plan had sprung almost fully formed into her mind. It was almost as if it had been a gift from God.

The gun had belonged to Chad, Jerry's best friend. Chad had no idea when or how Jerry had obtained the weapon, but he had held himself to blame for the "accident"—the kind gesture and word of a distraught friend. Ann knew the blame belonged wholly elsewhere. Jerry had left a suicide note: "I love her." That was all it said.

But to Ann it said everything.

"Hi, Ann," Sharon said, reaching the top of the hill, a bit winded from the climb.

"Hey, boss," Chad said, trailing Sharon.

"You're out of shape," Ann said to Sharon.

Sharon wiped her hand across her forehead and nodded. "Too bad I won't be able to let my fingers do the walking on our trip next week."

Ann spoke to Chad. "I thought you were at my house working on the wall."

"I have a class sixth period," Chad said. "You know that."

Ann glanced at Paul. "Somehow, I forgot."

Paul shrugged. "It was as good an excuse as any for my being late."

Ann wondered why he had lied to her about helping Chad with the wall. It wasn't the first time. She had caught him at it before. Usually his lies concerned trivial matters. They were almost always the sort that required little or no investigation to be found out. It worried her, his lack of discrimination, but since she lied every time she spoke to Sharon, she couldn't exactly come down on him about his lack of morality. Especially since she had never caught him lying to her about anything significant.

"Am I missing something?" Sharon asked Paul.

"We probably shouldn't get involved," Chad told her. "I've seen how people carry on when they're about to get married."

"Don't you think you should let me graduate from high school before you have me married?" Ann asked Chad.

He smiled at the remark. Except for his suffering over the loss of Jerry, he was a pretty happy guy, one of the few she knew. He was unlike his brother in every way. He was absolutely honest, incredibly patient. Nothing was too much trouble for Chad. He was an employee of hers, but he was also her guardian angel. She told him that once, and he had laughed, embarrassed. She was the only one he knew who looked like an angel, he replied. He had been telling her for months that she should marry him instead of his brother, but he was also one of the few people who supported her decision.

Sharon was at best lukewarm about Ann's marriage. Sharon didn't want her *rushing* into anything. If only Sharon knew what a rush she was going to get when the law came down on her.

"What are we doing this afternoon?" Sharon asked.

"Why?" Ann asked. "Don't you have to practice?"

"I always have to practice," Sharon said.

"I thought we might pick up a few things for our trip," Ann said. "It's only seven days away."

"I can get the stuff for the trip," Chad said. "Why don't we go get ice cream and see a movie?"

Sharon was interested. "I haven't seen a movie in ages. What's playing?"

"Horror films and sex films," Chad said.

"I think we should see two movies," Sharon said.

"Horror films always give me nightmares," Ann said, looking at Paul, who obviously didn't think much of the remark.

"There's one playing with a girl in it that looks just like you, Sharon," Chad said.

"If she looks like me then she's probably going to get killed," Sharon said.

Sharon often made derogatory remarks about her looks. Ann thought it was more out of habit than out of insecurity. Sharon had an interesting face. The line of her jaw was perhaps a shade too square, and her nose had a slight bump on it, but her smile was so winning and her brown eyes so warm that guys adored her. She definitely had a sexy body, and much of her allure lay in the way she used it to do the simplest of things, like crossing the campus at lunch. Although short—she was only five feet—she walked with a confidence that said she knew exactly where she was going. Inside and out, she came off as having her act together, and guys were not so threatened by this as women's magazines would have their readers believe. Many boys found her refreshing. She was asked out constantly. She seldom said yes. "I have to practice" was her usual reply. She hadn't even gone to the prom this year, although she had gone the previous year, with Jerry.

Sharon often put her own looks down, but she always praised Ann's. In this she wasn't alone, for praise came from all sides and was well deserved. Ann was not merely homecoming pretty. She had that rare face that movie producers and fashion scouts would cross oceans for. Like Paul, she had two different faces. If she tilted her head one way, she looked as innocent as the proverbial lamb, but if she turned it another, she looked ready for a night of naughty pleasure. Her eyes were cool liquid green, her lips pouty and red. People occasionally thought her long fall of dark hair was a wig, it was so fine and perfect.

But Ann's beauty brought her no pleasure. It was like her money. She felt it had nothing to do with the real her. It was simply something she was born with. That was another thing about Sharon's talent that had fascinated Ann. Sharon had also been born with her ability, but she'd had to perfect it with years of constant effort. Sharon had patience as well as determination.

Ann knew Sharon would need that patience while waiting for parole.

"Why would the girl die just because she looks like you?" Ann asked, thinking about Sharon's comment.

"I don't think I have the face for sequels," Sharon replied.

"Fred doesn't seem to agree," Chad said. "He keeps coming back. How's the romance climaxing?"

"Frequently," Sharon said.

Ann laughed with the others. She knew for a fact how sexually conservative Sharon was. Sharon's virginity said it all. On the other hand, Sharon had a nasty wit Ann never could match.

"Fred's coming with us, isn't he?" Paul asked. It had been Paul who had introduced Fred Banda to Sharon. That had been a couple of months before. Fred played guitar in a bar in Martyr, one town over from Wonderwood. Paul often stopped by the joint for a few beers, with the help of a false ID. Fred was also twenty years old. Ann didn't know a thing about him, except that he hardly talked and played a mediocre acoustic in a style that Sharon seemed to appreciate well beyond its true value.

"He wants to come," Sharon said cautiously.

"It's going to be hot next weekend," Chad said. "We'll probably have to swim naked in the river just to cool off."

"Sounds good to me," Ann said.

"Hey," Paul said.

"Are you bringing anyone?" Sharon asked Chad.

Chad smiled. "Yeah. You guys. Wasn't this trip my idea?"

Ann stepped to his side and put her arm around

him, feeling his ribs beneath his shirt. He was too thin. Maybe he wasn't as happy as he pretended to be. He could never gain weight and had never had a girlfriend.

"Chad's my date for next weekend," Ann said. "He's my last chance to party before his brother makes a proper lady out of me."

"Hey," Paul said again.

Chad hugged her in return. "We're going to have a great time."

They started down the hill a few minutes later. It had been decided they would just go for ice cream so that Sharon would have time for at least another eight hours at her piano before going to bed. Fame was waiting, they all agreed.

Ann and Paul lagged behind the others.

"She won't be physically hurt?" Paul whispered.

"Not unless the judge orders her hanged," Ann whispered back.

"How can you hate her so?"

"How can you love someone who has so much hate?"

"Don't play your word games with me!"

Ann shrugged. "I have a long memory."

"She's going to get off."

"That should make it easier for you to decide."

"I've already decided, damnit. Yes, I'll help. There, are you happy?"

Ann smiled. "I'm happy."

Her relief in that moment surprised her. Or perhaps it was simply surprise itself, unconnected to relief or otherwise. It *was* a bizarre plan. When she thought about it, she was amazed Paul had agreed to it. He must really love her. That was good. She was doing this out of love as much as hatred. She knew the two emotions weren't nearly so incompatible as people thought. They were like two sides of the same coin, the two ends of a torn rope that could one day be knotted.

CHAPTER
TWO

In the Courtroom

MARGARET HANOVER WAS THROUGH QUESTIONING Chad. John stood and walked toward Chad. Sharon leaned forward in her seat. She was hoping to get some points back right away.

"Hello, Chad," John said. "My name's Johnny Richmond."

"I know your name," Chad replied. He had regained a portion of his initial calm, but was still speaking softly.

"That's right. We met before. I stopped by Ann's place a few weeks ago. You were there, mowing the lawn."

He did?

Sharon had no idea what legwork John had done. He wasn't good at volunteering information. He liked to keep her in suspense.

"Yes," Chad said.

44

"You said a few minutes ago that you had known Ann Rice for ten years," John said. "Is that correct?"

"Yes."

"Did you like her?" John asked.

"Yes."

"Lately Ann's picture has been in the paper almost every day. She was a beautiful girl. She was extraordinary, really. Tell me, did you like her in a romantic sense?"

"Objection!" Hanover said. "Irrelevant."

"Sustained," Judge Warner said.

"But you did say you liked her," John went on without a pause. "Would I be correct in saying you wouldn't want her name tarnished?"

"She was my friend," Chad said.

"Just answer the question, please," John said.

"No. I wouldn't want her name tarnished."

"And you don't think she was suicidal?"

"She wasn't suicidal."

"Whose idea was it to go on this trip?" John asked.

"Like I said, it was mine."

"Actually, you said something slightly different." John took his notepad from his pocket. "You said, 'It was mine, I suppose. We all talked about it. I knew the area the best. Ann was excited about going.' That's what you said. Am I correct?"

"Yes."

"Did you all talk about it?"

"Yes."

"So you're not exactly sure who brought up the idea to go on the trip?"

"I believe it was me."

"Could it have been Ann?" John asked.

"I suppose."

"Was Ann a strong-willed girl?"

"Yes. She was very strong willed."

"Why did you camp where you did?"

"The spot has a nice view," Chad said. "But it's a hard climb to the top. Few people go there. It's a good place to go if you want to be alone."

"But who specifically wanted to camp there?"

"We all did. But the rest of the gang was mainly listening to me. I know that area like the back of my hand."

"You know it well because you regularly go rock climbing in the area?"

"Yes."

"But weren't you also giving Ann lessons in rock climbing? Prior to the weekend trip?"

"Yes."

"In that area?" John asked.

"Yes."

"In that exact spot?"

"We never climbed in that exact place, no, but near there."

"Chad, I feel that you are taking responsibility for many things that you had little to do with."

"How?" Chad asked.

"I've been watching you today. When you talk about that night, you act as if it was your fault. Also, I've studied your past. You've been having a hard time lately. I'm curious about your relationship with Jerry Rice, Ann's younger brother. Could you tell me about that?"

"Objection!" Hanover said. "Irrelevant."

"Your Honor," John said to Judge Warner. "I will demonstrate the relevancy. I need a few minutes."

"You may continue," the judge told him.

"Tell me about Jerry Rice," John said to Chad.

"He was my best friend. He died a year ago."

"How did he die?"

"He shot himself in the head."

"With a gun?" John asked.

"Yes," Chad said.

"With your gun?"

"Objection!" Hanover said. "The witness is not on trial."

"A minute, please," John said to the judge.

"Try to make your point," Warner said.

"Was it your gun, Chad?" John asked.

"Yes," Chad said.

"Where did you get it?"

"My father gave it to me."

"How did Jerry get ahold of it?"

"I have no idea."

"But you blamed yourself for his suicide. Why?"

Chad began to fidget again. "He was my friend. I knew he was depressed. I was with him earlier the night he died. I should have seen it coming."

"Was he the suicidal type?"

Chad lowered his head. "I didn't think so."

"But you say Ann wasn't either. Now both these people are dead. Do you think it's possible that one of them was murdered? That maybe Jerry was murdered?"

"Objection!" Hanover jumped to her feet. "The defense is trying to confuse the issue. Jerry Rice died a year ago. There was a thorough investigation into the cause of his death. He was found with the gun in his hand. The only fingerprints found, on both the gun and the shells, belonged to Jerry. There was not the slightest suggestion of foul play. Furthermore, the gardener at the time confirmed—"

"I was the gardener," Chad interrupted.

"Could someone have murdered Jerry?" John asked Chad quickly.

"Your Honor," Hanover complained.

"The witness may answer the question," Warner said.

"I don't know," Chad said, weary.

"You think he probably killed himself?" John asked.

"Yes."

John's line of questioning was confusing Sharon. He was jumping around, not focusing on specific points. He had brought up Jerry, of course, to give Ann a possible motive for committing suicide, but beyond that, she didn't know what he was doing. He told her once that he frequently ad-libbed while cross-examining. She understood now how serious he had been.

"I understand you were mentioned in Ann's will," John continued. "What did she leave you?"

"A few things, mainly books," Chad said. "I like to read. Ann had a lot of books."

Why did he bring that up?

"That's nice. Tell me about Ann and Sharon's relationship?"

"They were best friends," Chad said.

"Real close?"

"Yes."

"What about Sharon and Jerry's relationship?"

"What do you mean?"

"Did they have a relationship? Did they ever go out?"

Who has he been talking to?

"They went out a few times," Chad said.

"In the months just before Jerry died?"

"Yes."

"Did Jerry like Sharon?" John asked.

"Yes."

"Did she like him?"

"You should ask her," Chad said.

"What was Jerry depressed about?"

Chad hesitated. "I'm not sure."

"Come on now. You just said he was your best friend. Wasn't he depressed because Sharon wasn't interested in him?"

"Objection!" Hanover said. "Your Honor, we are not investigating the death of Jerry Rice. These questions are totally irrelevant."

"That's a *totally* ridiculous comment, Your Honor," John said, getting heated up. "We are trying to determine if Ann Rice committed suicide or was murdered. If we are to decide she killed herself, then we must have a motive. This is precisely what I'm trying to bring to light with my questions. I would appreciate it if I could do my job without being interrupted every two seconds. Jesus."

"There will be no swearing in this courtroom," Warner said.

"I'm sorry, Your Honor," John said.

Warner glanced at Hanover. "Defense may proceed."

"Thank you, Your Honor," John said. He took several steps toward Chad. "Was Jerry depressed because Sharon wasn't interested in him?"

"Yes," Chad said.

"Was Ann aware of this?"

"I don't know."

"You don't know? She was his sister. She must have known why he was unhappy."

"I'm not sure she did," Chad said.

John moved to where he could lean an elbow on the witness stand's rail. "You were close to Ann, Chad. It sounds like you were as close to her as her brother. Think carefully before answering this next question. Did you notice a change in the way Ann treated Sharon after the death of Jerry?"

Chad stopped. "Ann was a little cooler toward her."

"Did she blame Sharon for Jerry's death?"

Chad hesitated. "I don't think so."

"Whose idea was this trip?"

Chad sighed, distressed. "I don't know."

"Whose idea was it to go for the walk to the cliff?"

"Ann's. Sharon's."

"Whose?"

"Sharon's."

"What did Ann say just prior to Sharon suggesting they go for a walk to the edge of the cliff?"

"I don't remember."

John leaned forward. He was practically breathing in Chad's face. "Didn't Ann remark that the Milky

FALL INTO DARKNESS

Way would be more beautiful if the light of the fire wasn't in their eyes?"

Chad froze. "Yes."

"Didn't Ann, in fact, indirectly suggest with that remark that they should go for a walk?"

"I suppose it would depend on your point of view."

"Did you actually see Sharon push Ann off the cliff?"

"No," Chad said.

John turned away. "I have no further questions at this time, Your Honor."

When John was seated beside her, Sharon leaned over and whispered in his ear, "Well?"

"We still have a long way to go," he said. Across the aisle, Hanover stood.

"The prosecution would like to call Paul Lear to the stand," Hanover said.

CHAPTER THREE

SHARON McKAY ITCHED. HER ARMS AND LEGS WERE covered with tiny red bumps. There were five healthy human beings to bite on this camping trip, but the mosquitoes only wanted her. Chad said that was often the case. Mosquitoes could be real connoisseurs of blood. He knew a guy who had come back from a camping trip at Sunset National Park and had a swarm of mosquitoes outside his window every night for a month. Chad swore the mosquitoes had followed the guy home.

"It might be your deodorant attracting them," Chad said to her as they sat on a boulder beside Whipping River, their feet dangling in the cold, strong current. Sharon figured there must still be plenty of snow melting at high elevations. They could only wade a short distance into the river for fear of being swept away. Paul and Fred were lounging on nearby rocks, also cooling their toes. It had taken a hard five miles to get them this far. Ann had stripped down to a pink tissue-size bikini and was stretched out on a towel on a ledge a hundred feet farther downstream. The mosquitoes obviously didn't know that Ann was supposed to have the hottest blood to come out of Wonderwood High.

"I'm not wearing any deodorant," Sharon said.

"Maybe you should," Chad said in his most helpful manner.

"You're Mr. Expert Camper," Sharon said. "How come you didn't bring anything to keep the bugs away?"

"Oh, but I did." He dug in his backpack, which rested on the top of the boulder behind them. "I was just waiting for you to ask. I have two fine products. One is a spray-on." He handed her a tiny aerosol can. "The other's an oil."

Sharon studied the label on the aerosol can. "Warning: Do not spray in the eyes." The ingredients looked as toxic as an oil spill.

"Which works better?" she asked.

"I'm sure the oil does."

"You've used them before?"

"No. But you'll need me to massage the oil into your back."

"I don't have any bites on my back."

Chad smiled. "Not yet. You can't be too careful. I have great hands. Come on, roll up your shirt."

Sharon chuckled and turned her back to him, lifting the back of her shirt. She was a sucker for a good back rub. Playing the piano so much, her back and shoulders were often tight. Plus she liked flirting with Chad.

"Better watch your hands," she warned. "Fred might be watching us."

Chad glanced over his shoulder. "He's not. He's talking to Paul."

"I'm glad he's talking to somebody."

"Are you two not getting along?" Chad asked, touching his oily hands to her midback.

"Oooh, that feels good. No, I wouldn't say that. We don't really know each other, and it's become even more obvious to me on this trip."

"My brother seems to like him," Chad said.

"He's the one who introduced us."

"That's right, yeah. They were in the navy together."

"Were they?" she asked. "I didn't know that. I thought they just met at the bar where Fred plays."

"I might be confusing him with somebody else. I'm glad you're not wearing a bra, Sharon."

She giggled. The front of her shirt was creeping up toward her breasts. She didn't care. Chad *did* have great hands. Besides, it was nice to have a guy touch her, any guy, and she had always trusted Chad. She was tired of being Miss Pure and Innocent. She was glad she would be going to school in New York in the fall. She adored her mother, but she could be a bit of a drill sergeant sometimes, and this didn't make her an easy living companion. Her mom had been upset at the three days she was taking off to go on this trip.

"You won't be able to practice!"

And practice makes perfect, Sharon had reminded herself, groaning inside. It was not that she was tired of the piano, or that she wasn't excited about her scholarship. Getting it had been a dream come true. A thousand students had applied for each one selected. But she needed a break from the four to six hours a day she spent at her instrument. With her acceptance at Juilliard it had become even more imperative to her German teacher, Mr. Marx, that she constantly progress. No longer was she allowed simply to sit at the piano and play whatever came to her. Mr. Marx was not big on composing. Master the masters first, he said, and when she was his age she could try her hand at something new, forgetting that he was eighty years old.

Sharon liked Fred. He was by no stretch of the imagination an outstanding musician. She picked at her guitar maybe once a week for an hour or two and she could outplay him any day. But whereas her voice was enough to make ivory weep, he could sing in tune, and at least the songs he wrote were his alone, even if he wouldn't be attending this year's Grammys. The specifics of her attraction for him still eluded her, though. Ann didn't know what she saw in him, and it was true he didn't have a great physique. He was tall and gangly and walked with a slight stoop. His vision was awful, his glasses thick enough to be magnifying lenses. With his unkempt sandy hair and mustache, he looked very much like the starving artist he was.

His manner, however, had charmed her from the beginning. It was the very antithesis of his appearance. She knew he often pulled her leg with his extravagant compliments about her beauty and talent, but it was nice to be treated as a lady by someone who knew how to play the role of an English gentleman. The flow of his smooth words into her affection-starved ears was like the music of angels.

The first few times they had been together were great, but since then it had been hard to get much conversation out of him. Because those first meetings had been in the bar where he played, she suspected he'd been drunk then. Maybe the silent Fred she saw outside of the club and on the trip was the real Fred. But maybe he was just out of shape, and the hiking in the hot weather was wearing him down. He might be saving his breath for the next hill. It was four o'clock, and they still had a ways to hike. The plan was to camp at the top of the cliff five hundred feet straight up. Sharon understood it was a long way around to the top.

"I don't think we have to worry about the mosquitoes biting the front of my chest," Sharon said. "At least the male ones."

"Do I detect a hint of sexual frustration in that comment?" Chad asked. He wasn't just putting on the oil, he was digging deep into her muscles. She wasn't complaining.

"I wouldn't call it frustration," Sharon said. "It only bothers me when I think about it—all the time. Ouuh. Right there. Hard. Ouuh. Bliss."

"How are things with Fred in that department?" Chad asked.

"I can't comment on that." She added with a giggle, "But I wish I *had* something to comment on. Hey, what about you? Tell me about your sex life?"

He paused in the middle of his massage. "You know what they say about the fifth wheel? It's only good if there's an emergency."

"You don't feel like a fifth wheel on this trip, do you?"

"I'm the only one who doesn't have a date."

She glanced over her shoulder. Chad's face had always reminded her of a clown's, particularly with his big nose and bushy eyebrows, but she had happy childhood memories of circuses and clowns. She wouldn't have changed a thing about Chad. To look at him made her feel warm.

"Does that bother you?" she asked.

He smiled. "Only when I think about it—all the time."

She smiled. "Maybe you and I should get together."

"Really?"

She turned away. "Just keep rubbing my back and let me think about it."

He gave her something to think about. By the time he was done her back was humming. She wouldn't have minded if they were alone and he could have done the rest of her. Then again, she would have been too shy to take off her clothes. In a way, she was glad Fred hadn't made any advances in that direction. She wished she had Ann's lack of inhibition. She didn't want to end up an old maid. Music wasn't everything —it shouldn't be. Mr. Marx had never married, and look at him. He was always eyeing her mother's chest. It was sort of funny, but sad, too.

Chad had to help her up when he was done because she was so relaxed. Shielding her eyes from the glare of the sun in the clear sky, she looked at the ledge where Ann was sunbathing, a beautiful body in a beautiful land. With the noise of the rushing river Sharon was sure Ann hadn't heard them talking. Not that Sharon would have minded. She felt tired but exhilarated, at peace with the world. In addition to the back rub, the sound of running water had always had a tranquilizing effect on her. The air was warm and dry, but delightfully fresh and satisfying to breathe. She loved Utah. She loved this park. The glaciers had gouged out an exotic landscape while passing through the state thousands of years before. Whipping River flowed along a gorge as varied in design as it was in color. Shades of yellow, orange, and red combined to decorate the rugged contours of stone and earth. Every direction she turned it looked like a picture postcard.

"Ann has been as quiet as Fred on this trip," Sharon said.

"I noticed," Chad said. "She must have a lot on her mind."

"What do you really think of her marrying Paul?"

"I'm the wrong person to ask. I'm his brother. Besides, I want to marry Ann."

"I thought you wanted me?" she protested.

He started to laugh, but stopped short. He looked toward Ann. "I hope she's put on suntan lotion," he said. "She might burn."

Sharon studied him. There was something in his remark she found deeply touching. She didn't know what it was, except that his concern for Ann appeared so great that just the thought of her suffering a mild sunburn distressed him.

"I was wondering if she was mad at me," Sharon said.

"Why do you say that?" he asked.

"Sometimes I feel she blames me for what happened to Jerry."

He continued to stare at Ann. "Why?"

Sharon touched his bare arm. He was not wearing a shirt. He had an incredible tan. He was a whip of wiry brown muscle, although he could have used a few more pounds on his bones. He turned his sad brown eyes on her and her peace of a moment before wavered.

"Was I to blame?" she asked.

He frowned. "Sharon?"

"I don't mean to sound heavy. But you knew him."

"You knew him, too. I don't see how . . ." He stopped and shook his head. "You didn't have anything to do with it. I was more to blame than you. It was my gun, for Christsakes."

"But what does Ann think?"

"She doesn't blame you."

"Are you sure?"

He hesitated. "No one can be sure with Ann."

"Ain't that the truth."

Chad nodded in Ann's direction. "Go talk to her. Not about this, though. We're on vacation. I still think you're the best friend she's got."

"What about you?"

"I'm a boy. She's too pretty. I don't count." Chad pushed the tiny insect repellent spray can into her shorts pocket. "I used up all the oil on your back. You better take this. Oh, and I have another present for you." He pulled a knife from his backpack. "I just bought a new knife. I want you to have this."

"What for?"

"Protection. There are mountain lions in this park."

"Seriously?"

"The chances of running into one are slim, but take the knife with you if you go off by yourself. You can't be too careful. Be sure to sharpen it. The blade is dull."

The knife came with a leather case. She slipped it onto her belt and gave him a big hug. "That was a great rub. You're not bad for a fifth wheel. One day some girl's going to steal you out of the trunk and ride you till you go flat."

He laughed. "I won't hold my breath."

Ann didn't stir as Sharon approached. Sharon thought her eyes might have been closed behind her dark glasses. Sharon was on the verge of turning around and leaving when Ann suddenly spoke.

"We better be going soon," Ann said.

Sharon sat beside her, admiring Ann's lines and curves. God must have overseen the growth of Ann in the same way he had guided the sculpting of Sunset Park. Ann's mother had also been beautiful. Ann hadn't said much when she passed away a couple of years earlier. Ann hadn't said a word after Jerry's suicide. To this day Sharon didn't know if he'd left a note. She had been afraid to ask.

"Do we have to go?" Sharon asked. "Couldn't we just stay here?"

Ann sat up and removed her glasses. "Are you tired?"

"A little. I've been watching Fred. He looks exhausted."

Ann glanced over at Fred and Paul. They were throwing rocks into the middle of the river, talking together. Sharon was glad Ann was happy with Paul, although she had strong reservations about a permanent union between them. Paul was a babe, no question about it, but she pitied him trying to keep up with Ann for the rest of his life. Ann was no one to cross.

"He looks all right to me," Ann said.

Sharon smiled. "If you really want to camp at the top, that's fine with me."

"You don't mind?"

"No."

Ann nodded, her eyes focused on the churning water. "Is it cold?"

"It's like ice. It is melted ice."

"I wonder how deep the river is in the middle?"

"You should ask Chad," Sharon answered.

"Chad would know."

"Ann?"

"What?"

"Are you having a good time?" Sharon asked.

"Wonderful." Ann turned her big green eyes toward Sharon. She had an intimidating gaze. Sharon believed Ann had trained herself not to blink. Yet Sharon generally felt at ease in her company even though Ann lived in a twenty-six-room mansion with a waterfall in the backyard and Sharon lived in a two-bedroom apartment with a leaky roof. Ann had given her the shorts she was wearing. All the nice clothes Sharon owned had been gifts from Ann. Sharon wondered what she gave Ann in return, other than her music. Ann still loved to listen to her play. Ann could enter her practice room and sit for hours and not say a thing, and it wouldn't disturb Sharon in the slightest. Sharon believed she actually played better when Ann was present, with more feeling.

"Are you enjoying yourself?" Ann asked.

"I love the outdoors. I've been cooped up too long."

"That can be no fun. Thinking a lot about Juilliard?"

"All the time. I swing from imagining I'll dazzle everyone with my virtuosity to being sure I'll be expelled at the end of the first semester for lack of talent." Sharon paused. "I'm going to miss you."

"I'm going to miss you."

"Really?"

"Yes."

"I'll be home in the summer. We can talk on the phone." Sharon smiled. "You'll have to let me call you collect."

"It's a pity you won't be able to hook the phone up to your piano."

"I can send you tapes. Anything new that I write, you get to hear it first. How about that?"

"It wouldn't be the same."

"They have great recording equipment there. I'll sneak in and use it. It'll be almost the same."

Ann looked once again at the cold water. "Almost," she whispered.

"Did I say something wrong?"

"Not at all. It's just the mood I'm in."

Sharon lowered her head. She wanted to say something about how she'd gone to the cemetery the previous week and left flowers on Jerry's grave. It had been his birthday; it should have been his seventeenth. Sharon assumed Ann had seen the white roses; Ann must have wondered where they had come from. But Chad's warning came back to stop her. Poor Chad—he seemed lost now that Jerry was gone. The two had always been together. At least Chad's brother was here now. Paul had come to town two months before Jerry died.

Sharon missed Jerry. He had been like a kid brother to her. It got kind of sticky toward the end of his life when they dated a few times and he had gotten a crush on her. At the time, she hadn't realized they were dates. She thought she and Jerry were just going to movies as they had a hundred times before when Ann was with them. Fortunately, for her own peace of mind, they'd had a nice talk the last time they went out. He'd come away understanding that he was very important to her, and always would be.

Always. Almost.

He hadn't been upset with her, but he must have been upset with something.

Sharon sensed that Ann wanted to be alone. She stood. "I'll tell the others we'll be leaving in a few minutes," she said.

"Fine," Ann said. "Sharon?"

"What?"

Ann fiddled with the ruby ring on her finger. Sharon had given it to her as a birthday present. It always amazed her that Ann continued to wear it. The stone was tiny, nothing to look at.

"Let's talk later," Ann said.

"Sure," Sharon said.

Ann put her dark glasses back on and bent her head back, staring at the edge of the cliff five hundred feet above their heads. It jutted out from the peak at an odd angle, as if it were a distorted limb nature had tried and failed to break free. Any second now the sun would slip behind the cliff and leave them in shadow.

"We can go for a walk together under the stars," Ann said.

CHAPTER FOUR

In the Courtroom

PAUL LEAR AGREED TO TELL THE WHOLE TRUTH AND nothing but the truth. Hanover hardly waited for the leather-bound Bible to leave his fingertips before she was on her feet and heading for the witness stand. Paul sat stiffly with his hands clasped in his lap. Sharon squirmed. Paul definitely could not be counted on to be on her side. Beside Sharon, John was holding a pencil ready to take notes.

"What was your relationship to Ann Rice?" Hanover asked.

"I was her boyfriend," Paul said.

"You were much more than her boyfriend, weren't you? You were her fiancé."

"That's right."

"How old are you, Paul?"

"Twenty."

"How long had you been going with Ann?"

"About a year."

"Were you happy together?"

"Yes."

"Were you in love?" Hanover asked.

"Yes."

"What happened the night she died?"

"What Chad said."

"Could you tell us in your own words?"

"The girls got up and went for a walk," Paul said. "They headed toward the edge of the cliff. We couldn't see them. They were gone about ten minutes, and then we heard Ann scream the word *don't*. We ran to the edge of the cliff. Sharon was there, looking down. Ann was gone."

"I understand this must be very painful for you."

Paul shrugged, staring straight ahead.

"Whose idea was it to go for the walk?" Hanover asked.

"I don't remember."

Again, Hanover revealed by her body language that she had not received the answer she had expected. "Was Ann suicidal? To the best of your knowledge?"

"No," Paul said.

"His answers are killing me," Sharon whispered.

"Not at all," John whispered back.

"How did Ann feel about Sharon?" Hanover asked Paul.

"They were friends."

Hanover turned and headed back to her seat. "No further questions, Your Honor."

John stood and walked slowly toward the witness stand. It was John's way to make people wait for him. Paul followed him with his eyes the whole way. His expression remained difficult to read.

"How long have you been out of school?" John asked.

"A couple of years," Paul said.

"Where did you go to school, Paul?"

"La Mirada High. That's in California."

"Did you graduate?"

"No."

"Objection!" Hanover said. "Irrelevant."

"Your Honor," John said to the judge. "This was the deceased's fiancé. She was only eighteen. She was incredibly wealthy. The jury has the right to know why she had a fiancé at such a young age, and what he was like."

"You may continue," Warner said.

"Why didn't you graduate?" John asked Paul.

Paul shrugged. "School bored me."

"What did you do after you got bored with school?"

"I joined the navy."

"How long were you in?"

"A year and a half."

John scratched his head. "A year and a half, you say. I didn't know you could sign on for such a short period of time. I thought you had to be in for at least three years?"

"I received an honorable discharge."

"How did you manage that?"

"I have asthma," Paul said.

"When did you catch this?"

"I've always had it. But it began to bother me when I was on the ship for a long time. The fumes from the diesel engines aggravated it."

"How come the physical you received before joining the navy didn't reveal this condition?"

"I don't know."

"Did you tell the navy doctors you had asthma when you took your physical?"

"No."

"Did you ever see a doctor for your asthma before you joined the navy?"

"A couple of times."

"Who did you see?"

"I don't remember."

"You can't remember who you saw? Why not?"

"Objection!" Hanover said. "The defense is badgering the witness."

"I'm sorry," John told the judge, immediately turning back to Paul before the judge could respond. "What did you do when you got out of the navy?"

"I worked odd jobs."

"You did this for the last year and a half?"

"Yes," Paul said.

"Did you file income tax returns during this time?"

"No."

"Why not?"

"I was just working odd jobs. I didn't make that much."

"Where were you living?" John asked.

"Right after I got out of the navy, I was living with my mom in California."

"What brought you to Utah?"

"I came to live with my dad," Paul said.

"About a year ago?"

"Yes."

"That's when you met Ann?"

"Yes."

"Did you know about Ann before you came to Utah?"

"What do you mean?"

"Your brother worked for her. Did he tell you about her?"

"Sure," Paul said.

"Did he tell you how pretty she was? How rich she was?"

"I knew she had money."

"Did you come to Utah specifically to meet Ann?"

"No. I came here to find a job."

"You came all the way from Los Angeles, with its millions of people and thousands of businesses, to Wonderwood, Utah, in order to find a job?"

"I told you," Paul said coldly. "My father lives here."

John was pleased he had at last gotten a reaction out of him. "Were you broke when you got here?" he asked.

"I was pretty low on cash."

"Have you been working odd jobs in Wonderwood?" John asked.

"Yes."

"Like what?"

"I've painted a few houses."

"Whose house have you painted?" John asked.

"I don't remember the names of the people."

"Did you help your brother paint Ann's house?"

"Yes," Paul said.

"Is that when you met her?"

"Chad had introduced us before then."

"How long were you and Ann going together before you decided to get married?"

"Eight months."

"You decided to get married about four months before she died?"

"Yes."

"Why did you want to marry Ann?" John asked.

"She was a great girl."

"But didn't you think she was kind of young?"

"No," Paul said.

"What attracted you to her? In particular?"

"Objection!" Hanover said.

"Mr. Richmond," Judge Warner said. "Are you sure this is relevant?"

"I withdraw the question, Your Honor," John said, and he smiled. "But I do have another question. Tell us, Paul, how much did Ann leave you in her will?"

Paul glared at John. "I don't remember."

"It was a small fortune, wasn't it?"

Paul sat rigid. "It was a lot."

"Did you actually see Sharon push Ann off the cliff?"

"No."

John nodded. "I'm through for now, Your Honor."

The instant John was back in his chair Sharon was all over him.

"What are you doing?" she demanded. "You can't

prove Paul killed Ann. He wasn't anywhere near when she went off the cliff. Besides, he loved her."

John regarded her curiously. "You five made an interesting group. I wonder if you know who loved who. Or who loved what."

CHAPTER
FIVE

ANN STARED AT THE FIRE AND THOUGHT OF THE SUN, while all around her the night was dark and cold, even with her friends sitting by her side. She had told Paul they'd go to Mexico, but she had always intended to live farther south—in Honduras, perhaps. She liked the tropics, the heat. The hike to the top of the cliff had been sweaty, but the air in the mountains quickly forgot the sun once it was gone. Soon, in a matter of days, she would forget what it was like to shiver.

"It's like ice. It is melted ice."

Ann was afraid. She could hear the blood roaring through her ears, pounding, and she had to tell herself that no one else could hear it. She was talking to herself about a lot of things: the exact length of her rope versus the exact length of her fall; the distance the cliff stuck out from the rock wall; the strength of the harness she had on under her sweatshirt. These things she'd already thought through, but now her conclusions seemed less defined, more open to debate.

Chad had built the fire. He had collected a load of sticks the last three miles of their hike, while the rest of them had all they could do just to keep their legs moving. Chad had chosen their campsite, or he thought he had; it was the one he and Ann had used before when he'd been teaching her rock climbing. She had directed him to it with subtle hints.

A breeze came up out of the gorge from the direction of the lake below, but they were tucked at the base of a twenty-foot overhang. Still, the cold plagued Ann, and she wanted nothing more than to snuggle up beside the fire and sleep. Because she'd been thinking endlessly about her plans the night before, she hadn't been able to rest, and after the all-day hike, she was exhausted. And she had another long hike ahead of her before she could rest. She had to get back to her hidden car, which was not far from the lake, parked behind a cluster of trees at the end of a deserted dirt road. The thought of the effort to come, however, did not dissuade her. Nothing could. The memory of last August was still vivid in her mind. The red gobs of blood and white chips of skull—and Jerry's wide-open eyes, staring up at her in helpless sorrow, asking her, so it had seemed, where his life had gone, and why.

Why Ann? Why Jerry?

Then she had seen the note, but even that had provided no answer. There was no answer that could explain how a sixteen-year-old boy could one day be brimming with life and the next be dead. God had messed up pretty bad when he made people capable of loving other mortal beings. God had messed up in a lot of ways in Ann's opinion.

Ann had reviewed the specifics of the plan with Paul on the final leg of their hike, lagging behind the others, with only Fred behind them, who was apparently suffering from exhaustion. Ann had not liked having Fred at her back. She didn't trust him. He never said anything. He couldn't be that tired. She wondered what he wanted from Sharon. Ann was glad he wasn't her problem. She was almost glad for Sharon that Sharon was going to have bigger problems to worry about.

Paul had been in a foul mood. He had been complaining to her of all the things that could go wrong. Nevertheless, he had not tried to talk her out of jumping, and for that she was grateful. She needed his support. She needed his love. She had told him she loved him only minutes before they reached the top of the cliff. He stopped and looked back the way they'd come. Fred had been so far behind at that point that he wasn't even visible.

"Why do you love me?" he asked.

She had smiled at the seriousness of his question. "Because I need you. Because you need me. I don't know."

"Was there ever a time you felt you needed Sharon?"

The depth of the question had surprised her. She had seen no point in lying to him. "Yes. When I first heard her play." She put her hand to her head. "Jerry loved the way she played, too."

"Are you sure you don't need her anymore?"

She had nodded. Then he had kissed her and said nothing more.

Now they were singing songs. Fred had his guitar out. Sharon was playing it. Fred tried strumming a few chords, but they sounded the way all his music did, flat and uninspired. In Sharon's hands the instrument sang. Sharon had such beautiful hands. Although she was short, her hands were as long and elegantly shaped as those of the finest pianist. The gang was fooling around with old Beatles songs. Fred had finally consented to open his mouth. The beer Chad had dragged to the top of the cliff helped in that respect. Fred had drunk as much as the rest of them combined. He had taken to pawing Sharon between numbers. Ann only regretted she couldn't push him off the cliff before she jumped. She still didn't understand what Sharon saw in the guy.

Ann glanced at her watch. Ten-ten. Another few minutes and they should go for their walk. The coroner had placed Jerry's death at ten-thirty. It struck Ann as appropriate that she should appear to die at the same time. She was sure no one would make the connection.

"Do you know 'If I Fell in Love with You'?" Chad asked. He had been trying hard to join in the singing, but his voice was as weak as that of an owl with laryngitis. Yet he looked happy, and it was hard for Ann to look at his face and not feel sad that she would take that happiness away.

"I know the music," Sharon said, playing the opening chords. "Do you know the words, Fred?"

"What do you mean?" Fred asked, laughing. "I

wrote the words. Lennon and McCartney—we go way back."

"Funny, funny," Sharon said, giggling. She'd had a few beers of her own. Ann seldom drank. It made her lose control. She hated not being in control.

"I know all the words," Chad said. "I have them memorized."

"Then I'll play and you'll sing," Sharon said.

"Please don't," Fred said, shifting his legs and accidentally kicking the end of a stick buried deep in the fire, sending a shower of sparks heavenward. "I'm still digesting my dinner."

"That wasn't very nice," Sharon said, poking a playful elbow in Fred's side. "Apologize to Chad."

"Can I wait until he's done singing?" Fred asked. That was supposed to be a joke. He burst out laughing. Chad took it all in stride.

"I often sing it in the shower," Chad said. "That way no one can hear me." He cocked his ear to the night. "I guess the river isn't loud enough to save me from embarrassing myself tonight."

They could hear the river, faintly, sounding much farther away than it was. Ann could hear the cold in the splash of the water on the smooth stones. She could feel it in her blood. Her watch continued to tick, her heart to pound. She had held so much in for so long! It would hurt to let it all out at once.

Sharon will know. She will know when I scream.

But only half of it. Ann wouldn't have to fake her scream. It would be genuine. Her brilliant plan had not taken into account her brilliant fear.

"Why did you memorize the words?" Paul asked his brother.

"So I could sing them on your wedding day," Chad said.

"The fire's bright," Ann said suddenly, the sound of the words surprising even her. She had not meant to act so soon.

"It is," Sharon agreed. "It's wonderful."

Ann tilted her head upward. "But it makes it difficult to see the Milky Way."

Sharon set the guitar aside. "Ann, why don't we go for that walk now?"

It was too perfect. The time was obviously not hers to choose, Ann thought, not to the minute. The coroner could have been wrong about Jerry, anyway. Ann looked at Sharon through the flames and smiled. "All right."

Ann stood. Sharon did likewise.

"You girls want to be by yourselves?" Chad asked.

Ann nodded. "Yes," Sharon said.

"Remember where you are," Chad warned, also standing. "Don't walk too far in any one direction."

Ann looked down at Paul as she left, but she couldn't see into his eyes, not as she had done the first time they met. Maybe it was the light. She squeezed his shoulder. He nodded faintly.

"Take care, Ann," he said.

"I will, Paul."

It was Sharon who brought up the idea of walking to the edge of the cliff. "Maybe we'll see a shooting star," she said hopefully as they turned away from the fire and headed into the night.

The terrain at the top of the cliff was uneven. There were few loose rocks, but the ground rose and fell in grades up to four feet. They had to watch each step.

Brittle red dust crunched under their sneakers. Sharon had brought a flashlight; Ann purposely left hers behind.

It was only three hundred yards from the campfire to Ann's diving board. Moving a step ahead of Sharon, Ann carefully guided the two of them to the desired spot. The wind rose around them like the flapping of the wings of a gigantic prehistoric bird.

The cliff edge came to an abrupt halt, which worked to Ann's favor. Near the edge were several twisted and jagged bushes. Another bush stood at the exact edge. It was there that Ann had hidden the end of her rope. She had little fear of Sharon spotting it. Despite its precarious position, the bush had a full growth of leaves.

Sharon swept her light to the right and left. There wasn't a tree in sight. She turned the beam down, but it failed to illuminate any of the river below. Ann asked her to turn off the light, and Sharon did so. There was absolutely no light. Without the moon it was impossible to see anything in the mountains at night. Except for the stars. Sharon spotted the Milky Way and pointed it out to Ann.

"I wonder if they have music in heaven," Sharon said.

"If they do, then they've got a hell of a band," Ann said, referring to the sixties song about the many rock musicians who had prematurely met their deaths. Ann pulled her jacket tighter. Sharon wouldn't stand there long in that cold, Ann thought. Sharon continued to stare at the stars.

"I guess they've got plenty of keyboard players," Sharon said.

"There's always room for greatness," Ann said.

Sharon turned to her, her body an outline of shadow. "Do you really think I'm great?"

"I know you are."

Sharon laughed softly. "I wish I could believe you."

"But you do believe me. That's one of the things we have in common. We both know that if we have to, we can do anything."

"What do you want to do with your life, Ann?"

It was a simple question. Sharon had probably asked it as casually as she would have asked the time. But the effect it had on Ann was immense. She suddenly felt the need to know the exact time. She pulled her wristwatch close to her eyes, the hands glowing faintly in the dark. It read ten-eighteen, not ten-thirty. Yet out of nowhere, Ann felt—no, she *knew*—the coroner had definitely been wrong when he filled in the time of Jerry's death. Jerry had died before ten-thirty. It was suddenly as if Jerry were standing beside her and crying in her ear in pain, choking on his own blood as it poured into his lungs. The wind cried in concert with him as it slapped Ann's fine hair against the side of her head, feeling to Ann in that moment like an ethereal paw pounding on the door to her soul, begging her to stop the pain.

"I can't think of anything I want to do," Ann replied.

"Nothing?" Sharon asked.

"No."

"That's not true."

"It is." She stared down at the river she could not see. "It's cold."

"We should go back," Sharon suggested, a note of concern in her voice.

"You're right." Ann turned her back on Sharon. The gesture was largely symbolic. It meant nothing, really, not in the utter darkness that surrounded them on all sides. They were but wraiths of their former selves. That's how it would be from now on. That's how Ann wanted it. She realized then that there was another reason she was going to commit this foolhardy act. She wanted to get away from herself. Sharon was not the only one Ann loathed.

"Leave me the light," Ann said. "I'll join you guys in a few minutes."

"You don't want to walk back together?" Sharon asked.

"No."

Sharon slipped the light into Ann's hand. Then Sharon reached around with both arms and hugged her. "You are so important to me," Sharon whispered in her ear.

"Do you need me?"

Sharon let go. "Yes."

"That's good," Ann said.

Sharon left her. Ann let her go a ways before turning. She was counting. The seconds. Her heartbeats. The wind. The time it had taken Jerry to die from the time he had pulled the trigger. It could take a while to walk a hundred and fifty yards in the dark over rough terrain, half the distance to the campfire. Ann wanted Sharon only halfway there. She had to be careful. Already she could barely see Sharon.

When a minute had passed, Ann knelt by the bush, and turning her back to the campfire once again, flipped on the flashlight for a fraction of a second. The flash was good enough for her to locate her rope. Grabbing the end of it out of the thorny bush, feeling the cold sting of the metal clasp in the palm of her bare hand, and the coil of the second rope with which she would lower herself the final few feet to the river's edge, she turned off the light and threw it over the side of the cliff. The wind was blowing hard in a straight line toward the campfire. This was both good and bad. When she screamed, her voice would carry. If the wind had been blowing in the opposite direction, they might not have heard her. On the other hand, such a strong wind could push her toward the wall of the cliff as she fell. She couldn't risk falling straight down. She'd have to compensate for the wind by giving herself a running start.

Ann lifted the back of her jacket and sweatshirt and fastened the clasp at the end of the rope to a ring located in the center of her back, where the two wide straps of her elastic harness crossed. It was conceivable that the shock of her sudden braking would rip both her jacket and sweatshirt to pieces. At the moment, it was the least of her worries. She might have delayed too long before reaching for the rope. It was imperative that Sharon be out of sight of the others when she screamed.

What am I waiting for? I should scream. Now!

Yet she delayed several seconds more. The reason was simple. She was afraid, more afraid than when she had come home late to a strangely silent house disturbed by the faint smell of fired gunpowder and drying blood. She had tiptoed into the hallway toward her brother's bedroom, softly calling Jerry's name.

She kept waiting for him to answer, and an irrational dread filled her heart with each passing second when he failed to respond. Until she saw him. Then there had followed a moment of relief. Until she really saw him. Then she began to fall inside, even as she ran to him on the outside.

None of this was really new to her, she realized suddenly, and it sharpened her resolve. It gave her courage. That night, she had learned in a way she would never forget what it was like to fall into darkness.

Where was Sharon? Ann couldn't see her. But she could see the others, blurred black silhouettes against the campfire. Fred turned his head her way . . . and *maybe* toward Sharon.

"Don't!" Ann screamed.

And with that she turned and ran, and jumped, screaming all the way into nothing.

That is how it was for her at first. She existed in nothingness. She could not feel her body. She could not hear the wind. She could see nothing. This lasted for perhaps two seconds, but it was a long two seconds. Then a roar filled her frozen ears and a black landscape spun toward her blinking eyes. In an instant, she was shaken to the core by a sensation of incredible speed. She saw more than she could comprehend, her mind straining to keep up with her external velocity.

There was the river, reaching up toward her like a huge geyser shot from beneath the earth. That was exactly how it seemed—the river was rushing toward her as swiftly as she toward it. She saw the wall of the cliff, apparently inches from her nose, and the length and breadth of the entire gorge shrank before her accelerated vision. If she stretched out her arms, she felt she could touch both ends of it. Only she could not feel her arms. They had turned to leaden wings, which she struggled in vain to unfold. That had been part of her plan. To decrease her speed by spreading her body in the manner she had learned sky diving. Now it seemed nothing was going to slow her, not even the rope tied to her back. For the first time Ann wondered if she had made a terrible mistake.

She realized she was still screaming.

Ann saw one other thing while she fell. Winter Lake. She registered the sight with faint surprise. It had been invisible to her as she had stood at the top of the cliff beside Sharon. Perhaps her terror had sharpened her eyes. She remembered how the two bridge builders' bodies had been swept into the lake and lost. The memory brought her a pain similar to that of losing her brother.

But she suffered the memory only briefly.

The rope suddenly ran out. She stopped falling.

The jolt almost snapped her in two. Yet she did not register it in a purely physical way. In fact, the moment the jolt shot through her body, she momentarily lost consciousness. Or else her soul bounced out of her body for an instant. In either case, there was a short period of total disorientation, a painless period, followed by her first definite perception since she had taken her running jump.

She was not bouncing up and down at the end of the rope above the riverbank. She was exploding off the whipping end of the rope. She had gone too far with her running start. The wall of the cliff was not just beyond her nose—it was a hundred feet away. She had leapt too far from the wall and that meant she would be returning too quickly. Those were the laws of physics of a rubber band. She was being snapped back.

Ann realized just then that she was going to crash into the wall of the cliff with incredible force. As the roaring river rushed beneath her sweeping feet, she tried desperately to raise both her arms to brace for the impact. Two things impeded her efforts. First, the jolt had done a number on her spine, and her central nervous system was having a hard time communicating with the nerves in her arms. Her arms were coming up all right, but too slowly. Second, the jolt had also sent her spinning. One moment she was facing the wall, the next the rest of the gorge. In horror, she realized she might hit the wall with the back of her skull. In a flash, she saw the pillow on which she had found Jerry. It was so vivid, so real, she actually felt what it would be like to have the same pillowcase pulled over the top of her own head and tied tight.

Ann hit the wall. She hit it with her right elbow. The arm took the brunt of the impact, but the right side of her head also suffered a substantial blow. This time there was no loss of consciousness. The pure agony that swept through her body right then would not hear of it. She had shattered her arm. Bone went into nerve and set her blood to burning. She had screamed intentionally all the way to the bottom, and now she couldn't raise a whispered shout to save her life. Tears poured over her cheeks, and she pleaded and swore at

God to send her to the land of blackout. But he had never listened to her before; why should he start now?

She hung there, writhing, for maybe three minutes before she started to get ahold of herself. Any other girl would have taken three hours. She was intense, Ann Rice, but she was also tough. She had to remain calm, she told herself. She was hurt. She had broken her arm, and no doubt she had a concussion; she could feel the blood dripping over the side of her head. But she was alive. She had survived the fall. She was where she wanted to be—hanging some forty to fifty feet above the planet. It was not the end of the world, she thought. It could still be the beginning of her new life.

Paul?

Suddenly she had to stop talking to herself.

Far above, someone—and she knew it was not the wind—was fooling with her rope. It must have been Paul. He was trying to remove the pin. Or else he was trying to cut the rope directly.

What's wrong with him? Can't he feel the tension on the line?

Quickly, using her uninjured left hand, Ann unhooked the second coil of rope and attached the clasp to the ring on her harness. This was not so hard as it would have been had the jolt not also rearranged the harness to the point where the cross of the straps was halfway up her right side rather than in the center of her back. She didn't know the extent to which her clothing had been damaged—it was still very dark—but her jacket and sweatshirt appeared to be somewhere in the vicinity of her neck. It didn't matter. Nothing mattered now that her right arm was broken.

For in order to lower herself the remaining distance to the ground with the help of the second rope, she first had to undo the clasp of the first rope from her harness. To do this, she had planned to hoist herself up an inch or two with one hand while taking care of the clasp with the other. Now that was out of the question. She couldn't even move her right hand, much less ask it to perform a delicate operation in the pitch-black.

Minutes had passed since her jump, and Ann hadn't come to a halt yet. Swinging lazily back and forth over the river, she was brought cleanly above the water and the cold hard rocks at the high point of her arc. The icy spray of the rapids touched the warm blood flowing over the side of her face, and she had to struggle not to vomit. She was so dizzy!

Far above, someone took a firm hold of the rope and began to shake it violently. There was no question about what was happening.

But, Paul, I'm not down yet!

She was about to be cut loose.

CHAPTER SIX

WHEN SHARON HEARD ANN SCREAM, HER FIRST thought was that Ann was being attacked by one of the mountain lions Chad had mentioned. The possibility of a ferocious beast nearby didn't make Sharon hesitate in the slightest in going to her friend's aid. But if fear didn't stop her, the absence of a flashlight slowed her down. Spinning on her heels, she ran about thirty feet in the direction of the cliff before smacking her shin on a boulder, and falling flat on her face. Wincing with pain, she picked herself up. It was then Ann's screams ceased. Yet they didn't suddenly halt; the screams had trailed off in a way Sharon didn't understand. Nevertheless, the silence sent a chill through Sharon's body. She drove herself forward as best she could, feeling her way with her outstretched hands. It was so dark!

Sharon was lucky she didn't run off the edge. It was

the bush that brought her to a halt. She remembered the bush from a few minutes before, when she'd had her flashlight on and was talking to Ann. She hit a branch of the bush with her sore shin and stopped dead in her tracks. Fighting to catch her breath, she held her hair aside from the force of the wind and quickly scanned the area.

"Ann!" she cried. "Ann! Ann!"

There was nothing. Only the night. It was then the dark thought came into her mind, the thought that was so dark it made the outside seem like brilliant day.

She's gone over the edge!

Sharon fell to her knees and crept to the edge. A look down showed her only a black void.

"Ann! Ann! Ann!" She screamed again and again, finally closing her eyes, finally afraid of what she would have seen had there been light.

When she opened her eyes a moment later, Paul and Fred were crouched by her side with Chad standing behind them, a flashlight in his hand. In the harsh white of the light and against the pressure of the brutal wind, their faces looked grotesque.

"What happened?" Paul demanded.

"I don't know," she mumbled.

Paul grabbed her shoulders. "Where's Ann?"

"She's gone," Sharon said, pointing feebly into the abyss.

"I don't see her," Chad said desperately, spanning the immediate vicinity with his flashlight. "Where is she?"

"Are you saying she's dead?" Fred asked Sharon.

"No," Sharon moaned.

"Sharon," Paul said. "Just tell us what happened?"

"I don't know!" Sharon cried. "I think she fell off the side."

"No!" Chad also cried, beginning to tremble. "She couldn't have fallen. Ann! Ann! Ann! We've got to find her, Paul!"

"What happened, Sharon?" Paul repeated.

She looked up. In this nightmare, it was the same as looking down. "Ann said she wanted to be alone for a few minutes. I left her here with my flashlight. I started back to the campfire. Then I heard her scream. That's all I know, Paul, I swear it."

"Were you two fighting?" Fred asked. "We heard her screaming at you."

"No," Sharon protested. "I wasn't even with her when she cried out."

Paul stood. "Chad, give me your flashlight. All of you, stay here. Don't get any closer to the edge. I'm going to have a look."

"Do you think she's dead, Paul?" Chad asked, weeping.

"I have to look," Paul said, his hand out.

"Maybe she's playing a joke on us," Chad said, his voice cracking on a faint note of hope. "Maybe she sneaked around the campfire. Ann! Ann! Ann!"

"Give me the light," Paul demanded.

"Sure," Chad said weakly, handing it over. "Be careful."

Going down on his knees, Paul crept to the edge of the cliff, his light held out at arm's length. He didn't survey the side of the cliff long before he backed up and stood.

"I can't see a thing," Paul said. "But if she did go

over the side, there's a chance she caught a ledge. Here, Chad, take the flashlight. Run to the campfire. Get the rope. I'm going over the side."

"I don't think she could've caught a ledge," Chad said, anxiously shaking his head. "The chances of that aren't good."

Paul grabbed him. "Get ahold of yourself, man! She might still be alive. Get me the rope!"

"But we don't have enough," Chad said. "I didn't bring my full gear. We've only got a hundred feet."

"Just get it, damnit!" Paul ordered.

"OK," Chad mumbled. Taking the light, he turned and fled in the direction of the campfire. Fred took several careful steps toward the ledge.

"I don't see how she could have accidentally fallen off," Fred said.

"I wasn't with her," Sharon said, her voice pitiful in her own ears. She continued to kneel on the ground, sharp rocks cutting into her knees. "I was walking back. I left her my light."

"She might be all right," Paul said hopefully.

Fred leaned farther forward. "If she fell off here, she's dead."

Chad returned a minute later, a coil of rope in one hand and two flashlights in the other. "I should go over the edge, Paul," he said. "I have more experience rock climbing than you."

"No," Paul said firmly. "This could be dangerous, and you're an emotional wreck. Give me the rope. Where did you get that extra light?"

"I always bring this light," Chad said, turning it on and sending a powerful beam heavenward. "We might be able to see down to the river with it."

"I doubt that," Fred said.

"Give it to me," Paul said.

Chad handed over the rope and the stronger of the two lights. "I don't like this, Paul. This wind is bad. Let's just hike down to the bottom."

"That will take an hour," Paul said, kneeling and winding the end of the rope around the base of a nearby stone. "I've got to have a look over the side."

"We can use the light and look," Chad said, crying. "I know this cliff, Paul. What you're doing, it's not safe. Not without the proper equipment."

"I've used the light," Paul snapped, beginning to wrap the rope around his waist. "I didn't see a thing. Now stop whining and make sure this rope doesn't slip off the rock."

"Do you want me to guide you down with my light?" Chad asked.

"No," Paul said. "You'll just have it in my eyes. It's too weak, anyway."

"I really think I should go," Chad said desperately.

"Fred, give me a hand getting over the side," Paul said, ignoring his brother and tucking the powerful flashlight in his belt. "Sharon, help Chad hold the other end of the rope. Make sure it doesn't slip."

Sharon jumped up and tugged at the rope, which circled the waist-high boulder three times. Paul knew his knots. The rope was snug and secure. Sharon realized she was in mild shock. She was breathing. Her heart was pumping. But she wasn't precisely in her body. She was standing a foot outside it, watching, afraid to come back inside. She had gone on automatic pilot. Even so, she had enough sense left to be against Paul's plan. It was too risky, besides being totally in vain. Fred was right. If Ann had gone over the side, she was dead.

Why is Fred acting like I pushed her?

No, that wasn't fair. He had asked a couple of reasonable questions. Of course he must know she hadn't pushed Ann. No one could think that. It was impossible.

This is impossible! This can't be happening!

"I brought us here," Chad said miserably, his flashlight clasped tightly in his shaking hands. His face was as pale as death, his tears glistening like raindrops on a marble statue. The wind continued to blow, uncaring.

Paul went over the edge. Sharon held her breath as first his legs and then his chest and head disappeared. He was a brave man, she thought, a strong man. He was upset, but he hadn't lost control, even if he was acting rashly.

"Watch him," Sharon called to Fred, who stood close to the edge. "Chad, help me hold this rope."

"I can see him fine," Fred said, acting as a middle-man feeding the rope to Paul.

"The rope won't slip," Chad said, finally showing signs of life. He left her and crept to the edge. "But it might get cut on the edge. Fred, give it to me. You can't hold it like that. You have to wrap it around your own waist."

"Can we switch now that he's over?" Fred asked.

"Yes," Chad said. Stashing his light in his belt as his brother had done a moment before, Chad picked up the slack of rope that lay beside Sharon and the boulder and secured it around his waist. Then, in a quick, sure move, he took the tense end of the rope from Fred's hand.

"Hey!" they heard Paul call out.

"I've got you!" Chad called back, creeping to within inches of the edge. He obviously wanted to be able to look straight down while following his brother's progress. That in itself was extremely dangerous. Chad was having to lean into the wind simply to remain upright. If the wind was to falter suddenly, he—and maybe his brother, too—would be following Ann to the bottom.

Is that where she is? Is she already dead to me?

Sharon remembered the peculiar way Ann's screams had trailed off before stopping. How much more of an answer did she need? Yet she found it impossible to accept Ann's death, and it wasn't simply a matter of denial. Ann was invincible—Sharon had known that about her from the day they met. It should have taken an act of God to kill Ann.

"Do you see anything?" Chad called, cautiously measuring out six inches of rope at a time.

"No!" Paul called back.

"Come back up," Chad said.

"No."

"Maybe we should shine this other light below him," Chad said to Fred. "Take it out of my belt."

"He told us not to blind him," Fred said, leaving the light where it was.

"All right," Chad said, not happy. "Careful, Paul."

A couple of minutes went by. During that time, Sharon felt a jumble of emotions—sorrow, uselessness, impotence. Nevertheless, her sense of shock began to wear off and was replaced by cold hard reality. Paul would find nothing, and they would have no choice but to hike to the bottom of the cliff. There they'd find Ann's splattered body. There they'd have to figure out how to carry it back to Ann's truck. Really, when one got down to it, there seemed no point in going *there*. But it would have to be done. Sharon closed her eyes again. She began to pray. She didn't, however, pray that Ann was all right. She didn't believe God would bother with such an impossibility. She prayed that Ann had died instantly, and without pain.

"Do you see anything?" Chad finally called, not much of the rope left in his hands.

"No!" came back the faint reply.

"We're pulling you back up!" Chad called.

"No!" Paul shouted, from what sounded like a mile away.

"What's he doing?" Chad said impatiently. "He doesn't even have his flashlight on."

"Give him time," Fred said. "It's his girlfriend who's died."

"Don't say that," Chad snapped, upset. "We don't even know if she went over the side."

"All right," Fred said, obviously not believing a word of it.

"Turn on your light!" Chad shouted down.

"I dropped it," Paul called back.

"He dropped it," Chad said, fidgeting. "This is awful. This is terrible. We shouldn't have come here. I shouldn't have . . . Paul! I'm pulling you up!"

"Do it!" Paul shouted back, surprising them all.

"What?" Fred asked.

"He wants to come up," Chad said, excited, stepping back and planting his feet firmly. Chad showed remarkable arm strength in the speed with which he pulled his brother to safety. Paul was back up in less than a minute. Crawling away from the ledge, he plopped down and dropped his head in exhaustion, breathing heavily. Chad crouched by his side.

"Anything?" Chad asked.

"No," Paul said. "There was nothing." He raised his head and stared at Sharon, an odd expression on his face. "What did Ann shout before she fell off the edge?"

Why is he looking at me that way?

"I don't know," Sharon said.

"'Don't,'" Fred said, also staring at Sharon. "She screamed, 'Don't.'"

"What are you saying?" Sharon cried.

"Would you people quit wasting time," Chad said, gathering his rope up, his feeble flashlight all they had left to push the dark away. "We've got to start down."

Paul continued to hold Sharon's eye. It was then she understood. He *did* think she had pushed Ann off the cliff. He and Fred both did.

They've gone mad!

Yet Sharon saw no sign of madness or anger in Paul's eyes, and it made her wonder.

"Let's go," Paul said finally.

The hike to the bottom seemed to last forever. Their watches told a different story. They were at the base of the cliff in less than forty minutes. Chad's light had begun to flicker by then. They didn't need it, however, to locate the spot where Ann should have been. At Paul's instruction, they had left their campfire burning. Although the angle of the cliff wall prevented them from seeing it directly, the fire illuminated a trail of smoke as it rose into the sky, providing them with an accurate homing beacon.

But there was no body. Only the river, cold and powerful.

"Maybe she didn't go off the edge after all," Chad said for the third time.

"Would you stop that," Fred said. "You heard her as well as we did." He gestured to the river. "The current must have swept her body downstream. What do you think, Paul? Paul?"

Paul had taken the flashlight and was inspecting the boulders along the river's edge. Partially shielded by the rock wall at their backs, they felt little wind. Nevertheless, the cold spray of the foaming rapids dampened their faces, and a second roar, replacing the roar of the wind, filled their ears. Paul dropped to his knees, touching a rock with his hand. Chad took a step in his brother's direction.

"What is it?" Chad asked.

Paul quickly raised his head. "Nothing." He stood and rejoined them. "You're probably right, Fred. What should we do?"

Fred shrugged. "You're in charge here."

"We have to find her body," Paul said.

"Her *body?*" Chad asked, sliding in and out of reality. Sharon was worried about him. On the hike down, he had babbled incessantly about all the things he and Ann had talked about during the afternoon hike. Paul stepped to his brother and put a hand on his shoulder.

"She fell five hundred feet," Paul said. "No one could fall that far and live. I know she meant as much to you as she meant to me. But it's done. Her life is over. We both have to face that."

Chad's face collapsed. "It was my fault."

Paul hugged him tightly. "Don't say that. Please, don't ever say that again."

They began to make plans. Fred thought they should head back to the truck, all of them together. That would mean heading upstream. The lake, of course, lay downstream. But Paul wanted to stay and search for the body.

"It might not be that far from here," Paul said.

"It might be in the lake by now," Fred said. "What do you say, Chad? You know this area best."

"This gorge narrows as it approaches the lake," Chad said softly. "The last mile—it's treacherous. That's why we didn't come in that way. But splitting up might not be a bad idea. We should get to the authorities as soon as possible." He pointed south, at a ninety-degree angle away from the river, which ran west to east. Faint lights were visible in the far distance. "I could cut across the gorge and up onto the plateau. There's a campground there. Someone should have a CB."

"How far is that?" Fred asked.

"Five miles," Chad said. "But once I'm out of the gorge, the going's easy."

"How are you going to get across the river?" Fred asked.

"There's a bridge a couple miles downstream from here," Chad said.

"I still think we should go back to the truck," Fred said rather persistently for someone who had just said that Paul was in charge. Sharon had been waiting for a reassuring hug from him for the last hour. He was supposed to be her date, after all. Then again, she thought bitterly, if he believed she was a murderer, it was no wonder he was afraid to touch her.

"I think *you* should go back," Chad said.

"Are you saying Paul and Sharon should stay here?" Fred asked.

Chad shrugged helplessly. "If they want. They might find her."

"I'm staying," Paul said.

"So am I," Sharon spoke up.

"I don't think that's a good idea," Paul said.

"I'm staying," Sharon said.

"Why, for Godsakes?" Paul asked.

"Because she was my friend," Sharon said.

"It might be safer if she stays here with you," Chad said. "We have only one light. It's tricky hiking at night."

"Yeah, but is it safer for Paul if she stays here?" Fred asked.

"You sonofabitch," Sharon swore.

"What's that supposed to mean?" Chad asked, shocked.

Fred backed up a step. "I'm not saying nothing."

Paul raised his hands. "All right. All right. Things are bad enough as they are. Let's not fight. Sharon can stay here with me. Fred, you get to the truck." Paul held out the keys. "Here, take these. Drive to the nearest phone and call the police. Chad, if you find a radio, do the same. Tell the cops they might need to bring in a helicopter. Would it be all right with you guys if I kept the light?"

There were no objections. Chad set off directly

downstream. Presumably he would turn south toward the plateau once he reached the bridge. Fred turned west, upstream. Sharon didn't bid him farewell. He hadn't gone far, however, when he suddenly stopped and bent over, stooping in the shadows between two boulders.

"What is it?" Paul called.

Fred stood quickly. "Nothing," he said. He checked the ground once more, briefly, before turning and disappearing into the night, leaving Sharon alone with Paul.

"How are you holding up?" Paul asked, sitting down on a big rock, flicking off the flashlight, which was on the verge of dying anyway. They could hardly see each other. Sharon pulled her coat tight. It was a down jacket. The spray was beginning to soak in. They were going to have to move away from the river, or else she was going to freeze.

"I'll be OK," she said.

"You should sit down and rest."

"I'm not tired. Do you think I did it?"

"What?" he asked.

"Pushed Ann off the cliff."

"Of course not."

She relaxed a notch. "I didn't. That Fred—what a bastard he turned out to be."

"He's just upset, like the rest of us."

"Did you really know him in the navy?" she asked.

"Fred? No. Who told you that?"

"Chad did."

Paul hesitated. "No. Fred wasn't in the navy. But I met him when I was stationed in San Diego. He used to live there. He's not a bad guy."

"He's a bastard," she repeated. She took a step closer. She had not been able to read Paul the whole night, possibly because she could hardly see him. His voice gave away little. "How are you holding up?" she asked.

"I keep hoping it's all just a dream." He set his elbows on his knees and buried his head in his hands. "I can't believe this. Not Ann."

She wanted to touch him, comfort him, but she honestly didn't know him that well. "Should we look for her?" she asked gently.

He jumped to his feet at her question. He must be more tense than he was letting on. "I'll look for her. We only have this one light. To have any hope of finding her, I'll have to search close to the water. It would be too easy to break an ankle on these rocks. Come, there's a cave of a sort a hundred yards downstream from here. I'll lead you to it. Chad showed it to me. You'll be away from the spray. You can build a fire and stay warm until help arrives."

"But I want to go with you."

"Please don't argue with me. You'll just slow me down."

She gave in. She didn't want to cause him more grief than he was already suffering. He led her to the cave, which was not one a bear would have chosen for a winter of hibernation. It went in only a dozen feet, and had a low ceiling that forced her to crouch. Paul left her there for approximately ten minutes before returning with a pile of branches.

"They're damp," he said. "But they should burn. Do you have a lighter?"

She fumbled in her pants pockets. She had a small

jar of Vaseline, which she rubbed between her toes to keep them from blistering, and the can of insect repellent Chad had given her earlier. "No," she said.

He gave her his lighter. "I won't be gone long," he promised.

"What will you do if you find her body?"

He sighed. "I don't know."

CHAPTER
SEVEN

In the Courtroom

As Paul returned to his seat, Hanover stood. "The prosecution wishes to call Fred Banda to the stand," she said.

"Ah, your boyfriend," John said to Sharon.

"He's not my boyfriend," Sharon hissed. She had not forgiven Fred for the remarks he'd made shortly after Ann had died. When he had returned with the police, however, four hours after he had left her alone with Paul, he had been civil enough. He had even complained to the police that there was no need to handcuff her during the hike back to civilization.

But Fred hadn't visited her once while she was in jail.

"He's nothing to look at," John remarked as Fred shuffled his way to the stand, his stoop more pronounced than usual.

"He's a musician," she said. "I like musicians."

"You can do better," John said.

"With you?" she asked coolly.

John smiled. "Did I ever tell you what my favorite instrument is?"

"The harmonica," she muttered.

"Close. People. They're easy to play. I just have to open my mouth."

"You're disgusting," Sharon said. "Have you dug up anything interesting on Fred?"

"Oh, yes. Yes, indeed."

"What?"

"You'll see," John said.

Fred took a seat and was sworn in. He appeared to be suffering from the common sympton of not being able to look over at her. Hanover stepped up to him.

"What was your relationship to the deceased?" she asked.

"I'd met her a few times, usually when I was with Sharon," Fred said.

"Were you friends?" Hanover asked.

"No."

"What was your relationship to the defendant?"

"Is that Sharon?"

"Yes."

Fred glanced at her briefly now. "We were friends. We went out a few times."

"How many times?" Hanover asked.

"Six times, maybe."

"Were you romantically involved?" Hanover asked.

"Object!" Sharon whispered to John. "That's personal!"

"Shh," John said.

"Do you mean, were we sleeping together?" Fred asked.

"You object this instant!" Sharon told John.

"But I want to hear the answer," John said.

"Yes, that's what I mean," Hanover said.

"Not yet," Fred said.

John looked disappointed. "A big fuss about nothing."

" 'Not yet'?" Sharon muttered. " 'Not yet'? That guy has a lot of nerve."

"What happened when Sharon and Ann left the campfire?" Hanover asked.

"The girls disappeared in the dark in the direction of the cliff," Fred said. "They were gone a few minutes when we heard Ann shout the word *don't*. Then we heard her scream as she went over the cliff."

"No further questions, Your Honor," Hanover said, returning to her seat.

John stood slightly. "No questions, Your Honor."

Hanover looked over at John. She seemed to smile faintly—Sharon couldn't be sure. Certainly the woman was confident she had won.

"The prosecution rests, Your Honor," Hanover said, and sat down.

Judge Warner shifted in his seat. For the first time he began to show signs of the drowsiness John had spoken of. "The defense may call its witnesses," he said, and yawned.

John stood. "Thank you, Your Honor. The defense wishes to recall Chad Lear to the stand."

Chad returned to the witness stand, and the judge reminded him that he was still under oath. John stood and strolled in the direction of the jury, his manner casual, open, and friendly. Two middle-aged women on the jury brightened at his approach. Sharon couldn't see his face at that instant—he had his back to her—but she was sure John gave them a wink. John finally turned toward Chad.

"I want you to elaborate upon this coolness Ann felt for Sharon after Ann's brother had killed himself?" John said.

"I have nothing else to say about it," Chad replied.

"Why did you bring it up in the first place?"

"Because you asked me about it."

"I asked you if you noticed any change in the way Ann treated Sharon after the death of Jerry. The mention of a cooling in the relationship came from your side." John moved closer. "Did you ever see any sign, any sign at all, that Ann blamed Sharon for what had happened to Jerry?"

"You asked me that already."

"I'm asking you again."

Chad hesitated. "I don't think Ann blamed her."

"You hesitate. You hesitated the first time I asked. Why is that?"

Chad hesitated a third time. "Ann had a picture of Sharon and herself that she kept by her bedside. After Jerry's funeral, Ann got rid of it." Chad lowered his head. "She threw it in the garbage."

"She threw a picture of her best friend in the garbage?" John asked, raising his voice in case anyone had missed it. As a group, the jury leaned forward.

"Yes," Chad said.

"Did Ann ever ask you how Jerry felt about Sharon?"

"Yes."

"After Jerry was dead?"

"Yes."

"I can understand that. A guy will tell things to his best friend that he won't tell his older sister. Ann would have known that. What did you tell Ann?"

"That Jerry had cared for Sharon a great deal." Chad shrugged. "Ann was trying to understand why Jerry did it. But I wasn't trying to blame Sharon."

"I'm sure you weren't," John said sympathetically. "Did Jerry leave a suicide note?"

Chad looked at Sharon. "Yes," he said.

"What did it say?"

"'I love her,'" Chad said softly.

He loved me? He didn't love me. How could he love me?

Sharon felt sick, plain sick to her stomach. She felt sad.

Why didn't anyone tell me?

The answer was simple. Ann had made sure the information was kept from her.

John stopped directly in front of Chad. He rested a hand on the oak rail that enclosed the witness stand, not far from Chad's folded hands. He leaned forward, and when he spoke next, it was as if they were friends, alone and discussing private matters.

"She's gone, Chad," he said. "You don't have to protect her. Did Ann blame Sharon for what happened to Jerry?"

Chad closed his eyes and took a breath. "I think it's possible," he whispered.

"Ann was mad at her?"

"Yes."

John backed up a step, putting his hands on his hips, his whole manner changing in an instant. "Why was your brother only in the navy a year and a half when he signed up for three years?"

Chad's eyes popped open, startled by the strict tone of the question. "He told you. He had asthma."

"Didn't he also have a temper?"

"Objection!" Hanover said. "Paul Lear is not on trial."

"Overruled," Warner said.

"Your Honor," Hanover protested.

"I find the course of questioning relevant," Warner said. "The witness may respond."

"He received an honorable discharge," Chad said evenly.

"I have records," John said. "The jury may review them at their leisure while they are deliberating on their verdict. I obtained these records from U.S. Navy files. They record three separate incidents in which Paul Lear got into a fight with a fellow shipmate. One of these fights was with a superior officer. No wonder they let him have asthma. They wanted to get rid of him!"

"Objection!" Hanover said.

"Sustained," Warner said. "That last remark is to be stricken from the record. The defense will refrain from drawing conclusions."

"Sorry, Your Honor," John said. "Let's return to the night Ann died, Chad. How long did it take you to reach the edge of the cliff after you heard Ann scream?"

"Less than a minute."

"When you got there, what did you find?"

"Sharon," Chad said. "She was alone. She was kneeling near the edge with her eyes closed."

"Was she calling out for Ann?"

"She called out for Ann several times before we got to her."

"What happened next?" John asked.

"I scanned the area for Ann. I had the flashlight. I couldn't find her. We kept calling out her name. Then Paul wanted us to lower him over the side with a rope."

"Why?"

"He was hoping maybe Ann had caught a ledge as she fell."

"Was there any chance of that?"

"There was a chance," Chad said.

"But weren't you against Paul's idea?"

"Yes."

"Why?"

"I thought the chance was remote. Also, the wind was blowing hard. I didn't have the proper equipment. I thought it was a dangerous move."

"Did you try to talk Paul out of going over the side?"

"Yes."

"He was adamant?"

"He was upset. We all were. He was willing to take the risk if there was a chance in a million he would find Ann."

"How much rope did you have with you?"

"A hundred feet."

"How many feet was it to the bottom of the cliff?"

"Five hundred feet."

"So Paul knew before he went over the side that he was only going a little way down the side of the cliff?"

"Yes."

"How much experience did Paul have rock climbing?"

"Not much. I had shown him a few things when he first moved here."

"You were the expert. How come you didn't go over the side?"

"I wanted to. Paul insisted that he'd go. He thought I was in no shape to risk it."

"Were you?"

"I could have handled it."

"How many flashlights did you have at this point?"

"When I went back for the rope, I got a second flashlight. It was the most powerful one we had with us. I always bring it when I go camping."

"Did Paul take this flashlight with him when he went over the side?"

"Yes. He tucked it in his belt."

"Were you following him with the second flashlight?"

"No. I was feeding my brother the line. Paul didn't want a light on him. He was afraid it would blind him."

"For all practical purposes, wasn't Paul invisible once he went over the side?"

"No. I could see him the whole time. So could Fred."

"Could you see him clearly?" John persisted.

"No. It was very dark. All I could see was his outline."

"Why was that? Didn't he have his flashlight on?"

"He had it on at first. Then he dropped it."

"He dropped it?"

"Yes."

"When did he drop it?" John asked.

"When he was about thirty feet down."

"And after that, all you could see was his outline?"

"Yes."

"When you came to the stand the first time," John said. "I remarked that we had met before. It was exactly one week after Ann had died. I stopped by Ann's place. You were mowing the front lawn. You told me the district attorney had been by the day before."

"That's correct," Chad said.

John turned to the jury. "There was nothing unusual in this. The district attorney had a case to prosecute, I had a client to defend. We were trying to gather facts. Didn't we both stop by to talk to you about what happened that night, Chad?"

"Yes."

"But then you also let me go through a few of Ann's things?"

"You asked to go through them," Chad said.

"Yes, of course," John said. "But I wasn't invading her privacy. I just looked around the house. I went into her library."

"I remember," Chad said.

"And I found this book. Let me show you all." John retreated to his seat and removed a slim green paperback from his briefcase, which he placed on the table beside Sharon. John had never told her about his visit to Ann's house. He hadn't told her anything. John held up the book for everyone to see.

"This isn't the actual copy I found at Ann's house," John said. "I didn't feel I had the right to remove it. I bought this one at a bookstore. But it's the same book, isn't it, Chad?"

Chad leaned forward and peered at the cover as John held it out for him to see. "Yes," Chad said.

"Where did I find it?" John asked.

"In Ann's library, like you said."

"Where exactly in the library?"

"On the table beside her reading chair," Chad said.

"Do you know what this book's about?" John asked, studying the copy on the back cover.

"No," Chad said. "I haven't read it."

"It's about a girl who sets up her boyfriend for her own murder."

A hush went through the courtroom. Judge Warner jerked his head up—he had begun to nod off. The jurors looked at one another, muttering. Sharon's heart began to pound.

But what does it mean?

"The girl in this book arranged it so that she appeared to drown as a result of being shoved off a boat," John continued. "She fooled everybody. But she made one mistake. She took a friend into her confidence, and that friend betrayed her confidence." John stepped to the juror closest to the witness stand and handed her the book. "Why don't you pass it around? It's an interesting story. I'm sure Ann enjoyed it. She did read it, didn't she, Chad?"

"I thought I saw her with it," Chad said. "But I couldn't swear to it."

John turned from the juror back to Chad. "Then don't, since you've sworn an oath to tell the whole truth. But tell me this: When did you start to teach Ann how to rock climb?"

"A couple of months before she died."

"Was it her idea to learn?"

"Not exactly. I had been telling her for years how neat it was."

"But then, all of a sudden, she wanted to learn?"

"Yes."

"Was she very good at it?"

"Yes. She was fearless."

"When did you say you thought you saw Ann reading this book?"

"I didn't say."

"When was it?"

Chad paused. "A couple of months before she died."

"I have no further questions, Your Honor," John said.

"Does the prosecution wish to requestion the witness?" Judge Warner asked.

"No, Your Honor," Hanover said.

Chad stood and returned to his seat. John looked at Sharon, and she motioned him to come over. He obliged her.

"How am I doing?" he asked.

"What are you doing?" Sharon whispered.

"You'll see." He started to leave. She grabbed his arm.

"Are you saying Ann's not dead?"

John lost his cocky manner. He spoke seriously. "I'm sorry if I led you to think that."

"John?"

"I'm sorry," he repeated.

"Does the defense wish to call another witness?" Judge Warner asked.

John turned his back to her. "Yes, Your Honor. The defense wishes to call Sergeant Rick Patterson of the Salt Lake City Police Department to the stand."

The sergeant was a short round fellow, with a neck so fat and red it looked as if he had years ago inhaled a breath he had forgotten to exhale. He was not in uniform. Sharon always had trouble estimating the age of people who were overweight. He could have been forty, maybe only in his late twenties. He plopped down on the witness stand as if the exertion of walking from the back had worn him out. Sharon hadn't the slightest idea what he was doing there. John's tactics were really beginning to annoy her.

"What is your particular work for the police department?" John asked the sergeant when the swearing-in was complete.

"I work in auto theft," Sergeant Patterson said.

"Three weeks ago, on June twenty-third, one week after the death of Ann Rice, did your department find a stolen auto in Sunset Park?"

"Yes, sir."

"Tell me about it," John said.

"It was a brand-new Ford Taurus—in perfect condition. The vehicle ID number on the engine had been filed away. For that reason, we have no idea where it

113

was stolen from. We are still waiting for it to be claimed."

"How can you be sure it was stolen?" John asked.

"The filed ID number is a strong indication. Also, the license plate number was fake."

"Was there a key in the car?"

"There was one hidden between the muffler and the rear bumper."

"Where was this car parked?"

"In the vicinity of Winter Lake," Sergeant Patterson said.

"Did you dust the car for prints?"

"Yes."

"Whose did you find?" John asked.

"A number of fingerprints, as many as ten different sets. There were only two sets we've been able to identify."

"Who did they belong to?"

"Ann Rice and Paul Lear," Sergeant Patterson said.

A car? A getaway car?

A loud stir went through the courtroom. Sharon felt she was going to burst. Was Ann alive? That had to be what he was getting at. Yet that was impossible.

"Order in the court," Judge Warner demanded, slamming down his gavel. The bustle decreased but did not stop completely.

"How did you obtain a copy of Ann Rice's fingerprints?" John asked Sergeant Patterson.

"They were taken from her house."

"How did you obtain a copy of Paul Lear's prints?" John asked.

"They were already on file," Sergeant Patterson

said. "He had been arrested in San Diego on a drunk and disorderly charge."

"Thank you, sergeant," John said. "No further questions."

"Does the prosecution wish to question the witness?" Judge Warner asked.

Hanover turned and spoke to a young male assistant. The conference was brief. Hanover was clearly confused as to what John was up to.

"No, Your Honor," Hanover said.

"Your Honor," John said. "The defense wishes to recall Fred Banda to the stand."

Fred hurried back up front, standing straight and tall. He was jazzed up. They all were. The courtroom was alive with energy. John knew he was on a roll. He hurried to his briefcase and removed a small metal object. Sharon didn't have a chance to say two words to him before he was back up front. He held up the object for all to see.

"This is called a rock hook," John said. "Rock climbers use them. They are hammered into cracks in stone walls. Climbers then attach rope to them. I bought this hook at a sporting goods store on the way here this morning. Fred, have you ever seen one of these before?"

"Yes. I saw one on the ground the night Ann died. It was at the base of the cliff."

"When exactly did you see it?" John asked.

"It was after we had hiked down to the base of the cliff to search for Ann's body. When we didn't find her, and I was heading back to the truck to call the police, I spotted it in the rocks beside the river."

"Did you pick it up?" John asked.

"For a moment," Fred said. "Then I put it back where I found it."

"Did the others see you do this?"

"Chad had already gone downstream. Sharon and Paul saw me bend over. I didn't tell them what I found."

"You just left it there?"

"Yes," Fred said.

"But on the hike back with the police you began to think it might be important?"

"Yes."

"Did you tell the police about it?" John asked.

"No."

"Why not?"

"I figured I would tell them about it when we got there. But when we got there, the hook was gone."

"Why didn't you tell the police about it then?"

"I wasn't sure if I was looking in the right place for it. It never occurred to me that someone might have taken it while I was gone. I asked Paul about it later, but he said he hadn't seen it."

"Did you ask Sharon about it?" John asked.

"No. She was already under arrest."

"Thank you, Fred," John said. "I have no further questions."

Hanover stood. "No questions, Your Honor."

"You may step down," Judge Warner told Fred.

John took a deep breath. He had the momentum. He was not going to slow down. He faced the back of the courtroom. "The defense wishes to recall Paul Lear to the stand," he said.

Paul's reluctance as he approached the stand was

clear to everyone in the court. He moved with an exaggerated stride, as if he were forcing himself to look cool when he felt like gagging. His eyes had a strange combination of blank acceptance and repressed rage. He looked like a cornered animal. John had set Paul up well, even if the rest of them did not know for what.

Sharon's thoughts were in chaos. John was clearly trying to demonstrate a conspiracy against her between Ann and Paul, but he hadn't even hinted at the actual outcome of it. Or was this trial the outcome? Sharon told herself to be patient and listen.

What else can I do?

"Why did you go over the ledge?" John asked Paul after Paul had been reminded he was still under oath.

"I thought Ann might have landed on a ledge."

"That's crazy. You heard her fall all the way to the bottom."

"I thought there was a chance," Paul said.

"Why didn't you let Chad go?"

"He was too upset."

"Were you upset?" John asked.

"Yes. Of course."

"What did you do when you went over the side?"

"I looked for Ann," Paul said.

"With what? Your flashlight?"

"At first, yeah. I didn't drop it on purpose."

"What did you do after you dropped it? It was pitch-black. How come you didn't immediately tell Chad to pull you up?"

"I don't know," Paul said.

"How long were you over the side after you dropped the light?"

Paul's voice was even, although it was showing signs of cracking. "I don't know," he repeated.

"A minute?" John asked. "Five minutes?"

"I told you, I don't remember. It wasn't long."

"Was it Ann's idea to go on this trip?"

"It was Chad's," Paul said.

"Was it Ann's idea to camp on the cliff?"

"It was Chad's."

"Chad's! Was it Chad's idea to go for the walk?"

"Objection!" Hanover shouted. "The defense is badgering—"

"I'm just asking him!" John shouted at her, not even waiting for Judge Warner's OK to continue his barrage. For his part, the judge appeared fascinated. "It was Ann's idea to go for the walk to the edge of the cliff, wasn't it, Paul?" John asked.

"Maybe."

"There's no maybe about it. Ann was full of ideas. Wasn't she?"

"I don't know what you're talking about."

"Are you sure? You're under oath, young man. Everything you say is being recorded. If you lie, right now, you will perjure yourself. Do you know what that means?"

Paul nodded stiffly. "I know what perjury is."

"Why were your fingerprints on that stolen car?"

"It was Ann's car."

"Did she steal it?" John asked.

"She bought it. I don't know who from."

"Had you driven it before?"

"Yes."

"When?"

"A few days before we went on the trip."

"Did you ask what she was doing with a Ford Taurus? That's a fine car, but we're talking about a girl who owned a Ferrari and a Porsche."

"I didn't ask her."

"What was it doing parked near the lake?"

"I don't know."

"What did Ann do?" John asked. "Did she park it there the day before you guys went on your trip? Was she thinking of driving it home when the trip was done?"

"It's possible. I don't know."

"After she parked it there, what did she do? Walk home?"

"I don't know," Paul said.

"Did you go with her when she parked it there?"

"No."

"Are you sure?" John asked.

"No. Yes."

"Which is it?"

"I wasn't with her when she parked the car by the lake."

John held up the rock hook. "Have you seen this before?"

"No."

"But your brother taught you the fundamentals of rock climbing. You must have seen one of these before."

"I thought you meant that one in particular."

"So you have seen them before?"

"Yes."

"Did you see one the night Ann died?" John asked.

"Chad hadn't brought his equipment with him."

"You haven't answered my question."

"No."

"Are you sure?" John asked.

"Yes."

"What became of the rock hook Fred saw?"

"I don't know," Paul said.

"Did you see it?"

"No."

"It just disappeared?"

"I guess."

John set the rock hook down and fetched the thin green novel from the jury. "Have you seen this book before, Paul?"

"No."

"Did you ever hear Ann talk about it?"

"She talked about a lot of books. I can't remember them all."

John slammed the book down on the wooden rail of the witness stand. "I'm getting tired of this! 'I don't know. I can't remember.' That's all you have to say! You're acting like you weren't even there that night. Where did you go after you left Sharon?"

"I went looking for Ann."

"Did you find her?"

"No. Of course not."

"What were you looking for? Her body? Or did you know that she was still alive?"

The courtroom gasped. Sharon was no exception. She kept praying he would just come out and say if Ann was alive, despite the fact he had already told her that was not the case.

"I don't know what you're talking about," Paul mumbled.

"Yes, you do," John said, his face flushed with

excitement. "Ann hated Sharon for what happened to Jerry. Ann wanted revenge. Ann read a book about a girl who wanted revenge, a girl who set up a friend for her own murder. Then suddenly Ann took up rock climbing. Ann talked to Chad about planning a hike into the mountains. Then Ann bought a stolen car. Ann parked it in these same mountains. What did Ann do next, Paul?"

"I don't know."

"She talked to you! Ann needed you! What did you do when you went over the side, Paul?"

"Nothing."

"You did what Ann told you to do! What's the problem with jumping off the side of a cliff with a rope hooked to your back? Is it that your best friend might get blamed for your murder? Not for Ann. That was no problem for smart and pretty Ann. Ann *wanted* Sharon to get blamed. Ann wanted Sharon sitting in this courtroom. No, Ann had just one little problem she couldn't handle herself. It was why she needed you."

"No."

"Yes! Ann needed someone to cut the rope loose once she was down! What did you do when you went over the side, Paul?"

"Objection!" Hanover shouted.

"Shut up!" John shouted back.

"I didn't do nothing," Paul said weakly.

"You're lying to me!" John said. "You lied to Ann! How come Ann didn't make it to the getaway car? What happened to her? Were you able to find her? Did you meet her where you planned? Was she all right? Did you wish her good luck and kiss her goodbye? Did you tell her that now Sharon would pay? Or were you thinking about all that money Ann had left you? Were you thinking it would go twice as far if you didn't have to split it in half?"

"No."

"How come we can't find her body? Where is it? What did you do with it? How did you kill her, Paul?"

"I didn't kill her!" Paul suddenly cried. "I couldn't find her! She wasn't where she was supposed to be!"

John backed up a step. "Tell us about it," he said softly.

Paul stared at him, trembling. "I want a lawyer."

John turned away. "You need a lawyer."

John rested his case. Judge Warner called for final remarks. Hanover stood and spoke to the jury. She told them not to be misled by John's acrobatics, to focus on the facts. The only person who had been with Ann Rice when she went off the cliff was Sharon McKay. Paul Lear had nothing to do with it. Paul Lear was not even on trial, Hanover said.

John chose not to make any final remarks. He told Sharon it was unnecessary. He was right. The jury deliberated for less than thirty minutes before returning with a verdict.

Not guilty.

CHAPTER
EIGHT

WHEN SHARON HEARD THE VERDICT, SHE SCREAMED. IN the days leading up to the trial, she had repeatedly told herself that she would not cry if she was found guilty. She couldn't bear the thought of people pitying her. Her scream embarrassed her almost as much as tears would have. She immediately choked it off, but John was already laughing at her.

"What's the big deal?" he asked. "I told you we'd win."

"Does this mean I don't have to go back to that cell?" she asked.

"This means you can walk right out of here right now and buy me a late lunch."

"That's a deal!" She jumped up and gave him a big hug and kiss. Then she remembered who she was dealing with. She drew back slightly. "Just lunch? That's it?"

He smiled. "For this time, yeah. But you get in trouble again and it's going to cost you. Why are you shaking? You were never in danger of losing. I told you I was the best."

She hugged him again. "You *are* the best."

"Of course, if you really want to return the favor," he said. "I'm free for dinner."

She giggled. "Lunch is all you get. Oh, I don't know whether I should kiss you again or kick you! Why didn't you tell me what you were up to?"

"I didn't want to get your hopes up."

"You just wanted to keep me on the edge of my seat during the trial."

"I love an attentive audience," he admitted.

She stopped giggling. "I'm still not sure what happened. Did Paul kill Ann?"

"It looks that way."

"But he loved Ann," Sharon said.

"Yeah, sure. And Ann loved you." He saw the look on her face. "I'm sorry, Sharon. But sometime you're going to have to face the fact that Ann wasn't your friend."

"I can't believe it. How could you figure all this out?"

"I'm a genius," John said.

"No. Tell me."

"Finding the book was my first clue, along with the missing body. It got me thinking. And then Fred told me about the rock hook, and I kept asking myself what Paul was doing going over the edge. Then one afternoon, it all came together like an avalanche in my mind."

"I still can't believe this. Paul killing Ann? What do I do now?"

John glanced over his shoulder. The back of the courtroom was a swarm of reporters, all waiting eagerly with a thousand questions. She would probably get hit up for the movie rights of her life story before she reached the parking lot. She hated it. She hated people wanting to profit from someone else's hate.

Someone else's?

She couldn't attach Ann's name to the hate. Not yet.

"First find your mom and give her a hug," John said. "Then meet me out back and we'll go have fun."

"I want to bring my mother with me."

John laughed once more. "You are such an ungrateful young lady! Go ahead, go get her. I've got to make a statement about how corrupt the system is, and how I'm the only one who can save it." He gestured to Hanover, who was trying unsuccessfully to exit the courtroom through a wall of microphones. Her face was a mask of unhappy lines. She looked ready to commit murder. "Should I invite our beloved prosecutor to join us?" John asked.

"Let's not push it," Sharon said.

Before Sharon could find her mom in the mob, Chad appeared out of nowhere and tapped her shoulder. "Paul wants to talk to us," he said.

"Where is he?" she asked, jammed between ABC and NBC. Both wanted to know if she had ever been romantically involved with Paul Lear.

"Follow me," Chad said.

Chad led her through a door off the side of the

courtroom and down a long empty hallway. Sharon was surprised to find it deserted—considering the crowd they had just left behind—until she realized it was the hall she had taken to enter the courtroom. It was prisoners' road. They didn't belong there. But did Paul? Had they already arrested him?

Not yet, but close. They found Paul standing in the center of a small boxlike room that reminded Sharon of the room where she had first met John. Whether he was innocent or guilty, Paul was in for bad times. Chad and Sharon had to get by a police officer to speak to Paul. The officer was guarding the door. He had his hand on his gun. He said they could have five minutes.

"You didn't kill her, did you?" Chad blurted out before Sharon could even finish closing the door. Paul looked pained and angry.

"No," he said bitterly. "That lawyer's twisted everything inside out. I didn't do anything to Ann. I was just trying to help her."

"By cutting her rope?" Sharon asked, her own anger surfacing.

"Sharon," Paul said, his voice taking on a note of desperation. "You've got to believe me. I didn't want to hurt you. I was against this plan from the very beginning."

"What plan?" Chad asked.

"Ann's plan?" Sharon asked.

Paul nodded vigorously. "Yes. It was her plan. It was her plan to hurt you, Sharon."

"But why?" Sharon cried.

"Because of Jerry," Paul said.

"But I didn't do anything to Jerry!" she protested.

"That's what I told her!" Paul said. "But she wouldn't listen. She wanted to get you. She would have done anything to get you."

Sharon didn't absorb the blow easily. So it was true. "Is she alive?" she asked weakly. "Tell me if she's alive?"

Paul looked away. "I don't know. I honestly don't know."

"Paul," Chad said. "I'm confused. What did you do? What did Ann do?"

Paul wouldn't look at either of them. He spoke to the floor. "Ann wanted to set Sharon up for her murder. The lawyer got that right. Ann had a rope waiting at the edge of the cliff. When Sharon left Ann to return to the campfire, Ann hooked the rope onto a harness beneath her sweatshirt and jumped off the side. When she was down she was going to hike to the car and drive out of the country. She was going to disappear. We were going to get together in Mexico in a few months. That was the plan."

Chad frowned. "That's weird."

Paul nodded, disgusted at himself. "I can't believe I let her talk me into it. I must have been out of my mind. The lawyer was right about one other thing. Ann needed me to get the rope down for her. That's why I went over the side."

"Did you unhook the rope?" Chad asked.

Paul finally looked up. "I pulled out the pin. It was in tight—Ann told me it would be—but I had a big screwdriver hidden inside my jacket. Once I found the pin, I dropped the flashlight and used the screwdriver as a lever." He paused. "But I might have pulled it out too soon."

Chad gasped. "Before she was down?"

Paul nodded. "She had to use two separate ropes tₒ get down. The first one was measured to take her within fifty feet of the ground. When her fall was over she was supposed to hook the second rope onto her harness, unhook the first rope, and then lower herself the remaining fifty feet. It shouldn't have taken her more than two minutes altogether. I didn't even find the pin for at least five minutes after she jumped off the side. She should have been down!"

"Was there tension on the rope?" Chad asked.

"There was some, yeah," Paul said. "I thought it was just the weight of the rope. Five hundred feet can be pretty heavy. I was almost positive she was down "

"But you weren't positive?" Chad asked.

"No."

"Then why did you pull out the pin?" Chad demanded.

"I couldn't hang out there all night! The wind was banging me left and right. I was scared, all right. I was afraid your rope was going to snap. You guys kept yelling for me to come back up. It had been more than five minutes. I was just trying to help Ann."

"You keep saying that," Sharon muttered.

"It's true!" Paul said.

"But what if she hit the side of the cliff when she jumped?" Chad asked. "She could've been knocked unconscious. Then it wouldn't have mattered if you had given her fifty minutes. You could have cut her loose and dumped her in the river!"

Paul began to pace. The dimensions of the room didn't give him much space. He didn't realize it,

Sharon thought, but he was going to be spending a lot of time pacing whatever cell they put him in. She had done so.

"I know," he whispered finally.

"What is it?" Chad asked.

Paul suddenly halted and let his head fall back, closing his eyes. "There was blood, drops of blood— on the rocks beside the river. I saw them, Sharon, when I was searching for the wood for your fire. I washed them away. I didn't know what else to do."

Chad grabbed his brother. "It was Ann's blood?"

"Yes," Paul whispered.

"You killed her!" Chad cried.

"I didn't! For all I know, she could still be alive!"

"No." Chad shook his head. "She would have contacted you."

Paul turned to his brother. "You're right. I'm sorry. But you've got to believe me, I wouldn't have hurt her for the world. I loved her more than the world."

Chad shoved him away. *"You* loved her! *You* loved her! *I* loved her! I grew up with her! You're just some creep that wandered into town and killed her!"

Paul gazed at his brother in despair. "You're right."

"Are you the one that took Fred's rock hook?" Sharon asked.

"Yes," Paul said, his voice lifeless, still looking at Chad, who was bent over in a corner, tears rolling over his cheeks.

"But what about the rope?" Sharon asked. "Did you find that?"

"No," Paul said. "It must have washed away with her."

"You didn't see any sign of her when you searched downstream?" Sharon asked. "No more drops of blood?"

"Nothing," Paul said.

"She didn't make it to the car," Sharon said thoughtfully.

"No," Paul agreed.

"But why haven't they found her body?" Sharon asked.

"She was washed into the lake," Chad said bitterly from his place in the corner. "It's happened before."

"They still should have found her," Sharon said.

"I've been telling myself that," Paul said. "It's been a month. But she was going to call me, and . . ." He shrugged helplessly. "It's been a month."

I have to go back there.

The idea came to Sharon abruptly, but backed with firm resolve. She didn't understand the sense of it. What could she possibly find at the national park that the police hadn't been able to discover? Could it be she wanted to return to the scene of the crime to study the area to better understand how the crime had been committed?

Or to understand what the crime was?

That felt closer to the truth. Paul appeared to be telling the truth, but he'd lied to them before, and he was obviously very good at it. On the other hand, something else continued to gnaw at Sharon. It had bothered her the night Ann had supposedly died. It wasn't logical, but there it was nevertheless. It was the recurring conviction that Ann Rice would be the last of them to die. The feeling that Ann was invincible.

"I'm going back up there," she said.

"What for?" Paul asked.

"To look for her," Sharon said.

"You won't find her," Paul said.

"I'm going," she said. "Chad, will you come with me?"

"No," Chad whispered, still turned away and grieving. "I don't want to. I hate that place."

"But you know that place," Sharon said. "I need you."

"Ask me later," Chad said.

The police officer outside the door knocked. Their time was up. Before Sharon and Chad could even open the door, two other policemen entered the room. One held a pair of handcuffs. He asked Paul to extend both his hands. The other officer began to read Paul his rights. It was sad, Sharon thought. The loss of Jerry was sad. But Ann had made it worse for all of them with her crazy plan.

It was brilliant, though. I've got to give her that.

As they watched the door close on Paul, and heard the cuffs click tight, Sharon had another idea. It was more peculiar than the first, and far more disturbing. It concerned Ann's brilliance. Perhaps they had all underestimated her. Could Ann—believing that Paul had purposely tried to cut her loose too soon—have felt betrayed? And, feeling that way, could she have decided to get revenge on Paul Lear as well as on Sharon McKay? Maybe Paul was now exactly where Ann wanted him.

Ann could be alive.

CHAPTER
NINE

WHEN ANN RICE REALIZED SHE WAS ABOUT TO BE CUT loose, she also realized how close she was to dying. She was still swinging between the cliff and the river, but it was only at the far end of her swing that she was above enough water to cushion a fifty-foot drop. Otherwise, if she was dropped at the discretion of the person on top who was fooling with the rope, she was probably going to land on hard rocks, many of which were sharp. She understood in an instant what she had to do. With her broken arm, there was no possibility of slowly lowering herself with the second rope, even if she had all the time in the world; that was hard enough to do with two strong hands. Her only chance was to unhook the first rope—the long one that she had ridden to the base of the cliff—and fall when she chose. She had already secured the second rope onto her harness, and with it—at least until the first rope was cut loose—she might be able to save herself from drowning. It was her plan to drop into the middle of Whipping River.

That meant she had to hoist herself up an inch or two and detach the first rope from her harness. It meant she would have to use the hand on her broken arm to undo the clasp that tied her directly to the first rope—her right hand, which was now numb. If only she'd brought a knife! She could have cut the first rope as she swung out over the river. And she'd believed she had thought of everything!

Ann tried to flex the fingers of her right hand. They moved, a tiny bit, but it was as if they scraped the nerves in her right elbow as they did so. The pain was unbearable, and Ann had an extremely high threshold for pain. She wouldn't take a shot when she went to the dentist for a filling. Yet if it was unbearable, she told herself, she would make it bearable. She flexed her right hand again and bent her broken arm, actually hearing the bones crunch against each other.

Oh, God, am I so evil you'd put me through this?

She bit her lip. The blood in her mouth tasted like salt. She didn't have time to feel sorry for herself. God had nothing to do with her predicament. She had set all the pieces in motion, only it was a pity she hadn't been given the luxury of a practice run. She couldn't understand what Paul was doing. Why couldn't he feel the tension on the line? From the way the rope was jumping, it felt as if he was fighting with the pin. She had to act fast. On top of everything else, her swing was slowing. Soon the rocks would be her only choice for a landing spot.

Ann willed her right arm toward the harness. A

wave of boiling lava soared up her arm and into her brain, and she let out a whimper that sounded pitiful to her own ears. In the poor light, she could just make out when her fingers touched the metal clasp it was their task to open. Yet her fingertips did not register the touch; only her eyes did. Choking on the pain, she bent the fingers toward her mouth. She could not die. She would not die.

Ann bit into her fingers. They began to bleed, along with her lips and the side of her head, and this blood tasted both bitter and salty. Yet she felt the bite of her fingers, and that was something to be grateful for. She pressed them against the clasp and felt it, too, finally—a narrow steel band beneath a sticky smear, her blood. She grabbed the rope from which she hung with her left hand and looked down. She was swinging back out over the river. It was important she release just before she reached the far end of her arc. She began to count.

One. Two. Three!

Ann opened the clasp with her right hand, simultaneously yanking up on the rope, taking the pressure off the clasp. The hook at the end of the long rope slipped out of the clasp, and immediately she relaxed her left hand, letting go.

She began to fall, but this time it wasn't so far down that she had a chance to think, or even scream.

Ann hit the water at a favorable angle, feet first. However, because her sweatshirt, jacket, and long underwear were still bunched up around her neck, the water rushed over her bare stomach and chest and chilled her to the bone in an instant. She went down far—at least ten feet beneath the surface of the river—before her feet struck the bottom. It was horrible. She could see nothing. There was only cold pain and terrifying pressure. The current had her now, and she hoped her efforts hadn't been in vain. Maybe she should have stayed where she was. It would have been better to have her skull crushed than to drown. But it was no longer a question for her to debate. She had to breathe! She kicked upward.

The surface proved no friend. The moment she broke free of the icy blackness, she was pushed down again—then up again, and down again. The breaths she managed to draw between dunkings put as much water in her lungs as air. She started to choke. It wasn't hard to understand what was happening. Paul was still struggling with the pin. She was still attached to the first rope via the second rope. She had made another mistake. She shouldn't have hooked the second rope onto her harness. She was a dying fish flapping at the end of a five-hundred-foot line.

Ann could have died right then. It would have been a horrible end, but at least it would have been an end. But she refused to give up. Reaching with her left arm, using the rope, she began to pull herself toward the side, going against the full force of the current. She made it perhaps three feet before realizing it was hopeless. She was already exhausted, and the bank was forty feet away. Then she caught sight of a boulder, with dry land on top. It stood off to her left, farther into the river. Yet it was only ten feet away, and since she was on the verge of drowning, that counted for a lot. She pushed toward it with all her strength, primarily using her legs for propulsion. She reached it in seconds. The rear of the boulder sloped down to the water, and was equipped with numerous handholds, and she was able to pull herself out of the rapids and catch her breath. How wonderful it felt to simply sit and breathe and not have to choke.

She had hardly begun to enjoy the fresh oxygen when the rope fell from the sky and landed in a haphazard pile at the base of the cliff.

Way to go, Paul.

She would chew him out later, she decided. Now she had to get to the safety of the side before the others arrived, or before she froze to death—whichever came first. She was shivering something awful. Walking would help that.

It didn't take Ann long to formulate a plan of escape from the center of the rapids. Directly across from her, on the bank of the river not far from where she had relaxed in the sun earlier in the day, stood a particularly tall narrow boulder. If she could lasso the boulder—and she had plenty of rope to try—there appeared no reason why the current would not whip her over to the side. This way she could put the rapids to work for her.

Ann unhooked the clasp on her harness and put a small knot in the rope four feet from the end, before rehooking the clasp on the rope inside the knot, away from the end. The purpose of the knot was to prevent her lasso from tightening as she threw it out over the water, before it could reach the boulder. But she didn't make the knot so big that the clasp couldn't slip over it when she yanked on the rope.

Ann had two things going for her as she gingerly stood on the boulder and gathered together extra rope in her hands. It would take the others at least forty minutes to hike to the bottom. For all practical purposes, she could take as many shots at the boulder as she wanted. Also, even though her right arm was broken, she still had her best arm working for her.

Ann was left-handed.

Ten minutes later she caught her prize. It was good she didn't take any longer. The cold water had momentarily numbed her right arm, but the exercise brought it back to life, and each swinging motion caused her tremendous pain. Fortunately she made a bull's-eye hit on the boulder. Shaking the rope, her lasso settled all the way to the base of the tall stone. Things were finally beginning to go her way. The clasp slipped over the knot when she yanked on the rope, exactly as she had anticipated. It wasn't going to slip off. She wasted no time securing the rope around her waist. It would be good to finally be heading away from this place, she thought.

She jumped into the water.

It was cold, of course, but it didn't feel nearly so cold as the first time. Besides, she was only in it for two seconds. The current did its job well. A moment later she was standing dripping on the rocks that lined the river. She let the rope fall from her waist to her feet and felt wonderful to be finally free of it. The rope had begun to feel like a hangman's noose, dragging her down.

Yet she couldn't leave it where she had dropped it—she had to carry it away with her. She began to gather it into a coil around her neck. She couldn't believe how heavy five hundred feet of wet rope was.

She had carried the same rope on her back to the top of the cliff two weeks earlier, but she had clearly lost something between then and now.

Like four pints of blood.

Her head was still bleeding. Her cold bath had momentarily led her to believe it had stopped—wishful thinking. Losing blood was a serious matter, and she knew she had to try to stop it. But that meant pressing a cloth to it with her left hand, when she didn't have a cloth, and when she needed her left hand to brace her right arm. The latter was not improving. In fact, it was causing her so much pain that she began to give serious consideration to the idea of sitting down and waiting for the others to arrive.

I could tell them I accidentally fell off the side of the cliff and landed in the water and wasn't killed. It would sound impossible, but they'd have to believe me.

In the end, her pride, as much as her desire for vengeance, made her decide against the idea. She couldn't stand the thought of facing Paul and having him know she had chickened out. She'd have to go on. She'd have to suffer.

Ann set out downstream. Her first goal was the bridge. It lay approximately two miles away, one mile shy of Winter Lake. According to Chad, the bridge was seldom used. The neighboring terrain was fierce, and few people could even get to it. Also, the bridge hardly qualified as one. It was a rickety affair of rope and splintered boards. Fewer people dared to use it. It was not the same bridge that had cost the builders their lives years before. That bridge had never been completed.

Two miles. Walking that distance under normal conditions would have taken Ann less than a half hour. She had a brisk stride. But this two miles was equal to ten. She had to stay close to the river—the walls of the gorge gave her no choice. Without a flashlight, maneuvering between the rocks was difficult. But she didn't regret throwing the flashlight over the side before she jumped. Using it would have been too much of a temptation, and on a night like this, any kind of light would have been visible for miles.

She checked her watch. It was still working. The time was ten-forty. Twenty minutes had gone by since she had jumped. The others should be almost down the side of the cliff. Chad would be leading them down. He would be crying.

Don't think about it.

Ann plowed forward. Walking *did* help. It wasn't long before she stopped shivering. Plus she'd made a smart choice earlier in the evening when she'd put on her long woollen underwear. Even though it was wet, the wool helped to retain her body heat. She wished she could have said the same for her down jacket. The blasted thing was like a lead weight on her back. She would have taken it off and left it if she had not been afraid someone would find it.

She made fairly good time at first. She occupied her thoughts with how nice it would be to lie under a broiling tropical sun on a clean white beach and read about Sharon's murder trial in the papers. The fantasy served to pass the time and distract her from the pain in her arm. But when she finally caught sight of the roped bridge—a hundred feet above her head and spanning an exceptionally narrow portion of the gorge—the pain and extent of her injuries suddenly caught up with her. As she stared up at the bridge, it appeared to sway back and forth in the wind. Only she couldn't feel any wind; the surrounding stone walls blocked it. Except for the constant roar of the river, the air was still. It was she who was swaying.

Ann looked over her right shoulder, and it had surely been a subconscious fear that had kept her from doing so earlier. She had known she was still bleeding —it was impossible not to feel the sticky warmth dripping through her messy hair—but she had been fooling herself about how much blood she was losing. Her right shoulder and most of her right arm were literally soaked with blood. Her blood.

How much do I have left?

Ann felt suddenly dizzy. She had to stick out her left arm to brace herself on a nearby tree. The bark crumbled under her fingers. The tree was dead, and for some reason, the fact filled her with profound sadness. It reminded her of the way Jerry had died. All of a sudden, everything was reminding her of Jerry, especially the dark gook dripping out of the side of her skull. Her brains would drip out next.

I really should stop it. Soon.

An imperative thought, that drifted into her mind with dreamlike concern. She let go of her right arm and pressed her left hand to the wound. It felt lumpy and gross, and it hurt. Letting go of her right arm made that hurt worse, too. Everything hurt. Her head began to throb, pounding deep inside as if her heart had been transplanted into the center of her cranium.

Where was she? What was she doing? She had to get to the bridge. That was right. If she could just get up on the bridge, she could sit down, take off her jacket and sweatshirt, and rip the sweatshirt into long thin strips to make a bandage for her head. Down here, she told herself, next to this dead tree, she might die. It was dark down here. She had never cared for the dark.

I'm losing it.

The thought didn't help clear her brain.

A narrow stairway took her to the north end of the bridge. Lifting her legs up each rocky step, Ann imagined that she was back in a nightmarish civilization, riding an escalator to the top floor of a mall where all the stores sold pillowcases that had been dipped in blood. Her eyes saw red and black and nothing else, but a harsh white light began to mushroom inside her brain as her pain grew.

Should never have taken that running start.

Ann reached the bridge and stumbled to the center and collapsed.

Should never have thought of this stupid plan.

But she hadn't thought of it, not exactly. God had given it to her. Now God was trying to kill her. He had set her up. He didn't like her. He hadn't liked Jerry, either. Well, to hell with him. She wasn't going to die. She was going to live. All she had to do was tie her shirt around her head and squeeze her brains back into her skull, and she'd be able to think clearly again. Think about how evil Sharon was and how sweet Jerry had been before that goddamn bullet had permanently ruined his personality.

Sharp boards stretched beneath her. The sides of

the bridge were composed of four separate lines of ragged rope. Ann closed her eyes and leaned forward, resting her forehead on one of the ropes. She planned to rest for only a minute, but her lack of sleep and loss of blood decided otherwise. With Whipping River roaring deep and fast beneath her dangling feet, she blacked out. . . .

CHAPTER
TEN

*I*T WAS A DREAM. A DREAM OF WHAT SHOULD HAVE been.

Soft warm sunlight shone through yellow curtains. Music filled the air. Sharon was playing her piano. Jerry was singing. In real life, Jerry had hummed along when Sharon played, but he had a voice that only a mother could love. Yet here, in this magical place, his voice was divine, clear and strong, filled with love for Sharon and the promise of the time they had yet to live together. Seeing them happy, Ann felt great happiness. She felt love. Jerry was her dear brother. Sharon was her best friend. It would always be this way. The sunlight shining through the curtains was golden. They were in heaven.

But it was just a dream. Ann understood that even while dreaming. She didn't believe in a place called heaven. She knew it was just a state of mind, like a dream. Even so, she believed it could last forever. She felt if she could just touch the moment, if she could hold it in her hand, hold it tight, it wouldn't slip away. Therefore, she reached out to touch them, and Jerry stopped singing and Sharon stopped playing, and they turned toward her and smiled. Then they, too, reached out to her, as she hoped they would. But as she stretched out to embrace them, they began to fade, and another hand touched hers, a cold damp hand, and the warm sunlight dimmed and then vanished altogether.

Ann opened her eyes.

The stars were gone. So was the river. Gray stone covered the sky, dark shadows shifting across its rough surface beneath a dim wavering light. She was in a cave. She was not alone. Someone was at her side, holding her hand. Ann sat up with a start.

"How do you feel?" Chad asked.

Ann put her left hand to her head, taking her hand back from Chad. He had bandaged her head with a small towel. The pain remained, but the bleeding had stopped. She could think again.

"I'll live," she said.

"I found you on the bridge. You were about to fall off."

"How long have I been out?" she asked, her throat dry.

"I found you an hour ago."

"I see."

The depth of the cave was hard to distinguish. Chad had lit a squat kitchen candle and stood it on a nearby rock, but its feeble rays penetrated only a couple dozen feet before becoming lost in the darkness. Yet

Ann had the impression the cave went back a long way. It was definitely located near the river. She could still hear the roar of the rapids.

"What is this place?" she asked.

"I discovered it years ago," Chad said, watching her closely. "I was hiking. I come here occasionally. It's good shelter. You were bleeding. I thought I better bring you here."

"I'm lucky you found me when you did."

"Yeah."

She had to face him. She had to face the situation. "I guess you're wondering what I'm doing here?" she said.

"I brought you here."

"But I bet you didn't expect to find me on the bridge."

He hesitated. "No."

"What are the others doing right now?" she asked.

"Paul is looking for your body. Fred is hiking back to the truck to call the police. I don't know what Sharon is up to."

Something struck her as odd. "You don't seem surprised to see me," she said.

"I'm over my surprise."

"I bet." Ann gestured to the pile of rope that lay at her feet. "I suppose you've figured out what I did?"

He nodded. "You went over the cliff."

"But I didn't die."

"No."

She peered at him curiously. He was not reacting the way she would have expected. He was sitting very still.

"*Do* you know what I'm doing?" she asked.

"You can tell me."

"Before I do, you have to understand that I wanted to tell you a long time ago, when I first thought of it." She took a deep breath and glanced at the candle, its light reflecting in glittering snatches on the bare blade of the long knife he wore in his belt. Her only chance to go forward with her plan was to tell him about it. He had to understand how important it was to her. He had been loyal to her for many years now. He would at least listen.

"You were at the campfire when I went over the cliff," she said. "You heard me shout the word *don't*. That was to give everybody the impression that Sharon had pushed me." She paused. "I'm setting Sharon up for my murder."

"I understand."

"Do you know why?" she asked.

"Because of Jerry."

"Yes. You were there. You read his note. Sharon killed him."

"No, she didn't."

"Yes, she did. Jerry was your best friend. You know better than anybody what she did to him."

"Jerry loved Sharon."

"That's how she killed him. With her love. Love can kill just as easily as hate. I hate her, Chad. I want to kill her."

"Then why don't you?" he asked.

The question threw her completely off balance. It was so direct and to the point. It had never occurred to her. She *could* have killed Sharon. She could have pushed her off the cliff when they were alone together and then told everybody that Sharon had had an accident. It would have been so easy.

Why is Chad asking me this question?

"If I just killed her, she wouldn't suffer," Ann replied.

"You don't want her to suffer."

"I do."

"You care about Sharon," Chad said.

"How do you know?"

"I know you." Chad glanced toward the rear of the cave. Their voices echoed slightly as they spoke, even though they spoke softly. "I knew I would find you if I came this way."

"You mean, you knew you would find my body?"

He lowered his head. "Yes."

She touched his shoulder with her left hand. Her right hand had gone back to sleep, but her elbow continued to throb. Her blood had begun to dry on her coat. It was a sick sight.

"I'm sorry," she said. "I really did want to tell you."

"I understand," he repeated.

"Paul knows what I'm doing. That's why he went over the side of the cliff. He had to undo the rope. I'm supposed to be at the lake by now. I have a car there. With your help, I can still make it. I'm going to drive out of the country."

"No."

"Chad, please. There's no going back for me. She deserves what I'm doing to her. You've got to help me."

"No." He raised his head and stared at her. "The car won't work."

"Huh?"

"It's out of gas."

She took back her hand and frowned. "What are you talking about?"

"I didn't know if I'd be able to catch you before you reached the car."

It was cold in the cave—at best a candle gave off little warmth, and this one was on the small side. But the coldness Ann felt in her heart in that moment went far deeper than anything on the outside.

"How did you know about the car?" she asked.

"Because I know you, Ann. We grew up together. We think the same way. We're almost the same person. We should have been together." He shrugged. "But my brother had to come along."

"You knew about my plan?"

"Yes."

"Did Paul tell you?"

"No. I knew before Paul."

"That's not possible. How?"

"I knew your plan before you knew it. I gave it to you, Ann."

Ann froze. It was as if her heart had ground to a halt. She had to struggle to breathe. She couldn't speak. Chad was not expecting her to. His expression was strange. He was sitting at her knees, but it was as if he were regarding her from a great distance, a place of detachment. Nevertheless, the sorrow in his eyes was genuine.

"Everything you think, I think," he said. "It has always been that way. Don't you remember when we first met? Jerry introduced us. I came through the door, and you smiled at me and I smiled at you. We smiled together, at exactly the same instant." Chad smiled faintly. "I knew then that it was meant to be."

"What was meant to be?" she asked, not wanting to know.

"Us."

"There is no us."

He stopped smiling. "You don't understand."

"You're my friend, Chad."

His face darkened. "Is that all?"

"I thought that was enough."

He looked away and closed his eyes, taking a deep breath. He didn't seem angry, but he wasn't acting like himself. Ann was confused. Chad hadn't given her the plan. He hadn't said a word to her about it. Paul must have told him about the car. It was the only logical explanation.

Ann decided she should leave at the first opportunity. There was something going on here that wasn't normal.

"I knew I shouldn't have said anything," Chad replied finally. "I've felt that all along. I can read your mind, but you can't read mine. You can't see what's between us. It's been driving me crazy. But it has to be left unspoken. Talk about it and I wouldn't even get to see you anymore. That's what I told Jerry. There's no point in it, I said. Just keep your mouth shut."

"What about Jerry?"

Chad opened his eyes and held his fingers a fraction of an inch apart. "We are *that* close. The only thing that stands between us is our bodies. You're beautiful, Ann, but I don't care about that. It means nothing to me. You shouldn't care, either. So I don't look like Paul. Does it make that much difference?"

"What did you tell Jerry?"

"I'm a wonderful person, Ann."

"What did you tell Jerry!?"

Chad shrugged. "To keep his mouth shut."

Ann stopped. "About what?"

"Us."

That word again. "When?"

"Last August," he said.

Ann felt the coldness in her chest expand, filling her limbs, the life draining out of her. She saw *that* pillow again. She closed her eyes and still saw it. She opened them and saw Chad.

He had been the first one to find them, the first to comfort her.

"You killed him," she said softly.

He was watching her again. "Jerry killed himself, Ann."

"You're a liar."

The words stung him. He looked away again, toward the rear of the cave. He moved his lips, but no sound came from them. Or maybe she could no longer hear what he had to say. The roar of the river filled her head. It seemed to come from the rear of the cave as well as the opening. There was also a wind—the candle was suddenly flickering madly. But this roar, this wind—they were as much a part of her mind as of the surroundings. They beat upon all she had believed to be true and called it a lie. Chad *was* a liar.

Jerry did not commit suicide!

"He laughed at me," Chad was saying when she was finally able to understand him again. "He said I didn't stand a chance with you. I told him I knew that. I'm

150

not stupid. I'm a lot smarter than he was. He wouldn't let up on me. It wasn't fair. When he told me about Sharon, I always listened and gave him encouragement. But when it came to his sister—that was different. He thought he could say anything he wanted and get away with it. He was going to ruin everything. And after I had confided in him."

"How did you do it?" she asked.

He stopped and looked at her. "You don't want to know."

"How?" she repeated.

Chad looked pained. "I couldn't get him to promise to keep his mouth shut. When he went to bed, he said he'd have to think about whether he should tell you how I felt. He was being such a jerk. He liked the power he had over me. I drove home and got the gun my dad left. I came back. You know how I have the key. You were still at the movies with Sharon. Jerry was sound asleep. I could hear him snoring down the hall. I tiptoed into his bedroom. I had gloves on. I left the light off. He was sleeping on his back. He didn't feel a thing, Ann."

"What did you do?" she insisted, her eyes shifting back and forth between the knife in his belt and the candle on the rock. The knife was long. It was sharp. It would go deep into his chest if she shoved it hard enough. The candle was short. The puddle of wax around its tip was hot. It would blind him for several seconds if she threw it in his eyes.

Ann slowly began to open and close her right hand, trying to squeeze life back into it. The nerves at the ends of her fingers began to tingle. Her elbow continued to throb.

"I pulled his mouth open and stuck in the gun," Chad said.

"You pulled the trigger?"

"Yes."

"Just like that? You blew his brains out?"

"He deserved it."

Ann swallowed thickly, feeling a hurt deep inside that went far beyond anything her body had suffered since she had made her big leap. Just like that, he said. Bang. You're dead. Sorry for all the mess but I don't like you.

"How did you do the fingerprints?" she whispered.

"We had gone shooting the week before. His prints were on my shells. By the way, that was important. You can't put fingerprints on a shell after it's been fired. In suicide cases, the police always check if the prints are under the powder burns or on top of them. But putting his prints on the gun was easy. I just slipped it in his hand after he was dead."

"And the note?"

"Jerry wrote it. It was the beginning of a song he was working on."

"About Sharon?"

"Jerry wasn't really obsessed with Sharon."

Ann coughed weakly. "You wanted me to hate her. Why?"

"You wanted to hate her."

Ann trembled, realizing the enormity of her mistake. He was right. He had answered a question she had been asking herself from the beginning. Would her hate go away when Sharon was put away? The answer was no. Her hate had nothing to do with

Sharon. It was hers alone, and she alone decided in which direction it flowed.

Chad killed my brother!

She hated him. God, how she hated him.

Yet he hadn't really answered her question.

"But why did you want me to blame Sharon?" she asked. "Why her?"

"You started dating Paul last August. Even then I could see you two were serious."

She snorted. "You were jealous."

A note of anger entered his voice. "Does that surprise you? I'd known you for years. I'd taken care of your house. I'd taken care of you. I would have done anything for you. Then along comes Paul, and you jump into his arms. That bum. He hasn't worked a day in his life. He doesn't care about you. He just wants your money."

"You lie!"

"He told me so! Before he moved here, he used to ask me what you were worth. Your money's the reason he moved here."

"That was before he knew me!"

"He knows you now, and he didn't try to stop you from jumping off the cliff. You could have died trying what you did, and he knew that."

That stopped her. Not that she believed him, she told herself. She wasn't that gullible. Or was she? What was he getting at?

"What does Sharon have to do with any of this?" she demanded.

"I needed you to hate Sharon to bring you here, to this place, right now, under these circumstances. You look surprised. Don't be. Who gave you that book to read? Who taught you to rock climb so that you would lose your fear of heights? Who told you about the two men who fell in the river and disappeared? Who planned this trip? You may think it was you, but it was me. In the last year, I've given you a thousand suggestions telling you how you could get back at Sharon. Your ears heard them, your subconscious heard them, but your ego wouldn't let you recognize they were coming from me. This brilliant plan of yours—it was mine, all mine. I *made* you think it up. You see how well I know you?"

"Why did you do this?" she asked.

He had been cocky while explaining how he had manipulated her. Now he was embarrassed. He turned away, once again looking deep into the rear of the cave. Something about that area continued to draw his attention. The cold draft that disturbed the candle was coming from there. Ann didn't mind. The flickering flame created more wax. She was going to seal his eyes tight. Her left hand presently hung beside the rock on which the candle stood. Unfortunately, it was her right hand that was closest to the knife. Her best chance of grabbing the knife when she threw the wax in his eyes would be to use her right hand. She would only have a moment, and it would be pitch-black. She knew she would not have a second chance.

He's going to try to kill me.

Since he had told her about Jerry, he would have to silence her. The realization didn't bother her as much as another might have expected, probably because she had every intention of killing him. But she had to ask herself what she was waiting for, why she didn't just reach for the candle. She supposed she was curious as to his motives. She still couldn't get over that he had been behind it all. He had always seemed so *nice*.

"Why did you give me the plan?" she had to repeat, still slowly flexing her right hand. Feeling had returned to her thumb and index finger. Her palm began to tingle.

"You should know," he said.

"Out of revenge? You wanted to get back at me?"

"You wanted to get back at Sharon."

"Because I thought Sharon was responsible for the death of my brother! What did I ever do to you?"

His anger returned. "I'm sure Paul asked you the same question when you told him of your wonderful plan. What did Sharon ever do to Jerry? The answer is nothing! But that's what made you hate her so! She didn't do anything for him! And after he loved—" His voice cracked. His anger faltered. He dropped his head. "And after I loved you."

She spat out the words. "You don't love me."

"I do."

"Then why have you hurt me so much?"

He clenched his fist into a rock-hard ball. He looked at the knife in his belt. But he spoke quietly. "I've been suffering. You have to suffer, too. We have to do it together."

"That's the craziest thing I ever heard."

He nodded. "I *am* crazy. So are you. There isn't another girl in the world who would have done what you did tonight. But you did it. I knew you would do it. You're as crazy as I am."

Is that true? That can't be true.

Actually, Ann couldn't think of anyone else who would have taken such a jump. He had made an excellent point.

"But you didn't have to kill Jerry," she said, and now her own voice began to break. "He was your best friend."

"He was nothing to me," Chad said. "Paul is nothing to me. He betrayed me. He knew I cared for you, and he took you for himself. I know the lawyer Sharon will most likely be assigned. He's smart. He'll figure out what you guys were up to. I'll help him. I'll help whoever she gets to defend her. They'll break Paul. Sharon will get off. Paul will go to jail." Chad shivered and pulled his coat tighter. His eyes strayed to the side of her head, the blood staining through the towel. "It's cold in here. It's damp. There are many nights I've slept in here. The cold keeps you awake. I would lie awake and think of you lying here beside me."

"Bleeding?" she asked, her tone sarcastic.

"I didn't want it to be this way."

Ann decided she had better change her tactics. She would have to distract him as she reached for the candle and the knife. She had a basketball net at her house. They had played a lot of one-on-one games together. She was no slouch, but Chad could beat her with one hand tied behind his back. He was quick as a snake.

But he would let me win half the games.

Killing him was not going to be easy. Even if she got the knife. Five minutes of intense hate could not wash away a lifetime of trust. Ann deliberately caught his eye.

"Why didn't you just tell me how you felt?" she asked.

"It would have made no difference."

"Yes. It would have. I've always cared for you."

He chuckled without amusement. "As a friend."

She spoke gently. "Maybe we could have been more than friends."

He met her gaze. "Don't lie to me, Ann."

"You still love me, don't you?"

"Yes."

"Then love me."

He sniffed. "I have to kill you."

She smiled. "You have to kiss me first."

He blinked. "Why?"

"You have to kiss me goodbye." She leaned forward as if she were going to kiss him, carefully raising her left hand toward the candle, slowly moving her right arm closer to his knife. "Because *I'm* going to kill you."

The words were no sooner past her lips than she attacked. Grabbing the candle presented no problem. She had it in her left hand in an instant. Her swift movement almost put out the flame. A small portion of the wax spilled onto her flesh between her thumb and index finger. Chad could *not* read her mind. She had caught him completely by surprise. He stared at the flame even as she tilted the candle in his direction. He blinked once more. She threw the hot wax in his eyes.

The candle went out. She had expected it. The

darkness was absolute. But she didn't need light to hear Chad cry out. His hands shot up to his eyes—she heard them. She reached for the knife. Here she ran into a snag. Her mind could not override the sharp pain that shot up her arm from her elbow. She let out her own cry. But she would not let the pain stop her. Twisting on her side, she purposely rammed the top of her head into Chad's face. From the feel of it, she caught him square on the nose. He toppled backward and she pounced on him, straddling him with her knees. She didn't waste time striking him again. The knife was all that mattered. She only had to poke him once with it in a vital spot, and that would be the end of it.

It took Ann several seconds to get to the knife. By then Chad had recovered sufficiently to punch her in the jaw. He couldn't have outweighed her by more than twenty pounds, but he was a strong devil. The punch sent her thoughts reeling and her head rolling. Fortunately, at the same moment, her left hand closed on the hilt of the knife. More out of instinct than by conscious decision, she pulled the knife out of his belt and slashed it across his abdomen.

Ann had seen Chad sharpening his new knife on a stone earlier in the day when the group had relaxed by the river. He kept the blade razor-sharp, and in that respect she was lucky. Also, the struggle had caused the front of Chad's jacket to fall to the sides; she had an open shot at his guts. Had she only pressed down a bit harder with her slash, she might have mortally wounded him then and there. On the other hand, as it was, she caused him a great deal of grief. His scream as she crossed his belly with the knife cleared her head as well made her ears ring. It was loud.

"Ann!" he cried, his arms falling limp at his sides.

Ann twisted the knife in her left hand, pointing the blade straight down. Now all she had to do was plant it in the center of his chest. His heart would burst. His blood would spill out and soak the floor of the cave. He would bleed as Jerry had bled. He would bleed more. It was justice.

It is vengeance.

She should have wanted it. She should have found the taste of his blood sweet. Half an hour earlier, knowing what she knew now, she would have. But something had happened to her between then and now, since she had realized her year-long hate for Sharon had been without reason. It was almost as if something inside had snapped and made her weak, or perhaps clicked inside and made her wise.

There's no reason for any hate.

Ann realized she could not kill Chad. She had known him too long. He had been her friend, even if he was crazy. Yet this didn't mean that she was going to let him kill her. Ann set common-sense limits on any sudden revelation, particularly when her life was at stake. He was wounded. She had the knife. She should be able to escape. Jumping up, leaving him on the floor of the cave, she decided to give him one last present to make up for what he had done to her life. She kicked him hard in the side. He groaned.

"You know, Chad," she said. "I wasn't really going to kiss you. I wouldn't have kissed you if you were the last slime left alive on the face of the earth."

Ann staggered for the opening of the cave. She had to get back to where she had jumped. She had to talk to Sharon and Paul. She had to get to the police!

Stepping outside, Ann noticed it wasn't as dark as it had been earlier. She hadn't told Paul the literal truth when she had said that it would be a moonless night. The moon was simply to rise late. A milky white glow shone in the eastern sky, and she was happy for it. Finally she would be able to see where she was going.

The cave was situated up high, in an uneven stone wall that rose almost directly above the river. The way down was steep, but at least there was a way—not as safe or as smooth as the stone steps she had taken to the end of the bridge, but serviceable. Chad had brought her across the bridge, she realized, and way above it. She was on the south side of the river. That was both good and bad. It was bad because she wasn't sure which way the bridge lay, to her right or her left, and she would need to recross it if she were to have any hope of reaching the others tonight. It was good because the bridge was held together with old rope, and she had a sharp knife.

Ann glanced over her shoulder before she began her descent. Naturally, she couldn't see Chad; she couldn't see a dozen feet into the cave. Yet she felt a pang of guilt, a stab of fear. He might be bleeding to death on that miserable stone floor this very second. Or he might be climbing back to his feet with murder on his mind. There was no time to lose. She pressed on.

Ann had not gone far when her strength began to fail her again. Her nap in the cave had obviously not given her body enough time to replenish her blood supply. She had a phenomenal headache; it was as if the bones in her cranium were being welded together. Her lips were parched and bleeding. The night seemed full of blood. Her earlier dizziness returned. She half expected the moon to rise in the east dripping blood. One thought gave her strength.

The world is going to know my brother didn't kill himself.

The route down was tight and damp. She wasn't far from Winter Lake; she could see its wide dark shape off to her right. Here the rapids narrowed and the spray rose high on the cliff walls. Twice she lost her footing and almost took the short way down. Each time a handy branch saved her life. She wondered if God wanted her to survive. She was beginning to believe in him again, and to pray instead of curse.

It was her proximity to the lake that made Ann decide Chad must have carried her downstream from the bridge. The deduction was a calculated one, but a gamble nevertheless. Her pace was miserable. She couldn't stop glancing over her shoulder. Now she was kicking herself for not having at least slashed his legs. Her anxiety grew in proportion to her weakness. Fortunately, from what she could see, there was only one way down from the cave. He was not going to be sneaking up on her.

Ann finally reached the water and turned west, upstream, back toward the others. By then the moon had peeked over the horizon and she had light enough to plant each step wisely. For all it mattered. The stones were slippery, loose; her ankles twisted right and left inside her boots, adding to her pain and exhaustion. She was thirsty, but she dared not bend over and drink. She was afraid that she wouldn't be able to stand back up. Or that Chad would choose that moment to pounce. The farther she walked, the more convinced she became that he was on her tail. She could feel his eyes following her, his lovesick gaze that asked nothing from her except the sacrifice of her brother and the slitting of her throat. She tightened her grip on the knife.

He couldn't have carried me that far. I have to hang on.

Ann spotted the bridge ten minutes later. She was wrong. All told, Chad must have carried her close to a mile. She must not weigh as much without her blood. The nearness of safety brought her a needed burst of energy. The hundred-foot vertical hike back up to the bridge took her only three minutes. Ann actually broke into a smile as she stepped onto the flimsy walkway that stretched across the river. Pausing to catch her breath, she checked behind her, finding no sign of him.

"I'll tell them all, Jerry," she muttered. "I'll take out full-page ads in every goddamn paper in the state."

Ann started across the bridge. It swayed with each step forward that she took, and *that* was no hallucination. She ran her fingers over the rope that made up the handrails, feeling the prickly deterioration of the twine. A few slashes with her blade and it would be history.

Another spell of dizziness hit Ann as she reached

the far side. She was forced to her knees, slumping to the ground with half her body on hard rock, the other half still on the bridge. Her eyesight blurred, and she forced herself to focus on the moon, which now hung several degrees above the horizon. She couldn't remember when the moon had last had rings around it. Or a crooked grin on its face.

Cut these ropes and you can black out and it won't matter.

Ann sucked in a breath and raised her left hand, pressing the knife to the rope, beginning to saw up and down. Considering she was almost comatose, it wasn't too hard. Fresh strands popped up with each pass of her blade, and a minute later the rope snapped. Ann moved to the next rope, scooting her bottom clear of the bridge. She began to smile again. She hoped Chad was following her. What a surprise he would get when he saw the bridge hanging in the rapids. She could sit there all night and laugh at him across the water.

There were four ropes on each side. Ann took care of one side before moving to the next. The second group of ropes took longer. Three times she had to pause to rest. The knife might have been dulling. Her brain cells definitely were. Now the man in the moon was smoking a cigar. His smoke drifted across the sky above her head.

Those are clouds, you idiot. Keep cutting.

The bridge went down at exactly half past the witching hour—twelve-thirty. Ann noted the time for posterity. The crash of the flimsy boards on the hard rocks below was music to her ears. The water took ahold of what was left of the bridge and hurled it against the opposite cliff wall. The ropes on the other side would not last long against that force. Maybe later this summer she would find pieces of the bridge while sailing her boat on Winter Lake.

Ann realized she would not be leaving the country.

She sat against a boulder and laughed softly. She was through for the night. She would not be hiking back to the others. But they would find her in the morning—someone would. There would be a full-scale search for her body, and they would find her alive. It was cold, but summer was coming. She wasn't going to freeze to death.

"I did it," she whispered and let her head drop back, glad it was finally over.

It was sad. Perhaps she had cursed God too many times in her short life and he was still mad at her. The night was far from over.

Ann heard a sound below her. Footsteps.

"Paul?" she said softly.

A shadow was coming up the rock steps on *her* side of the river.

"Fred?" she called.

It was impossible to tell if it was a man or a woman.

"Sharon?" she said.

"No," a voice replied.

Chad!

Ann woke up fast. She leapt to her feet and held her knife ready. Her heart shrieked in her chest. The shadow paused on the next to the last step. She drew back her knife to strike.

Then a white light exploded in her eyes and she was blinded.

"I had one more flashlight no one knew about," Chad said.

"Turn it off!" she screamed at him, trying to shield her eyes with her knife hand.

"All right," he said. The light went off. The dark returned, and now it was filled with spots. One of the spots was Chad but she couldn't tell which one.

"Don't come any closer!" she said.

"All right."

"I'll kill you!"

"I don't think so."

"I swear I'll kill you!"

Time. A few seconds. My eyes will clear.

"You couldn't kill me half an hour ago," he said.

She took a step back, blinking, listening for his approaching feet, for a change in the distance of his voice. The spots were beginning to fade. All she had to do was stall him a few moments longer. Then she could slice him in two.

"You think I'm too nice?" she said, trying to sound confident. "What about that nasty cut I gave you?"

"It wasn't very deep, Ann. I'm here, ain't I?"

She hesitated. "How did you get here?"

"It doesn't matter."

"But I destroyed the bridge. How did you get here?"

"It's a secret."

"Did you reach the bridge before me?"

"No."

A twig crunched.

"You stay right there!" she shouted, holding her knife out.

"I want to talk to you, Ann."

She nodded. She was beginning to pick him up. He was the elongated blur ten feet in front of her. "We can talk," she said. "What do you want to talk about?"

"I don't want to hurt you."

She snorted. "Gimme a break."

"I don't want you to have to suffer," he said.

"If I just killed her, she wouldn't suffer."

Who had said that? She had said that. Christ.

"You just want to kill me," she said.

"Yes."

Ann blinked again. There he was! He was only five feet away!

"Stop!" she cried. "I'll poke you in the heart!"

He moved a step closer, taking on more and more detail. There was something odd about him. He was dripping with water! But that was impossible. He couldn't have swum across the river. He would have drowned. No one knew that better than she.

Ann glanced over her shoulder, the water churning a hundred feet beneath her like the foam of a breaking tidal wave. He was purposely backing her up against the river. He was smart. Let the water do the dirty work. Well, she wouldn't play that game. She planted her feet firmly.

"You're in pain," he said sympathetically.

"You're right." She drew back the knife. "And you're a pain in the ass."

He took another step forward. The moonlight caught his eyes. They were both bright and dark. They shone in the light of the moon, but as they stared at her, they seemed to devour her light. A wave of nausea swept Ann's body. She had not been there that night, but she recognized the look Chad must have worn when he stuck the tip of his pistol in her brother's mouth and squeezed the trigger.

"He was nothing to me."

"I love you, Ann," he said.

"I love you, too, you bastard!"

Ann swung at him. Under better circumstances she probably would have done him damage. But she was spent. She missed, and her momentum carried her around in a half circle before she could regain her balance. Nevertheless, she regrouped quickly and was on the verge of taking a second stab at him when Chad flicked on his flashlight for the second time. It was a dirty trick. She instinctively threw up her hand to shield her eyes, and in doing so, took one step too many backward.

Ann slipped. She fell. Almost off the side.

Chad caught her by the ankle, with her head hanging upside down above the roaring rapids. What was left of her blood rushed to her brain, and she felt as if the man in the moon was putting out his cigar between her eyes. Her skull exploded with pain.

"I'm going to pull you up," he said. "Don't fight me."

Ann still had the knife in her hand. "All right."

He began to pull carefully on her leg. The rock of the cliff wall scraped against the side of her head. Ann braced herself for one last effort. If she failed, he would kill her, and not only her. He would kill many others in his life. He was that kind of nut. They had nothing in common, and she didn't care what he said. He would probably try to kill Sharon.

Ann thought of Sharon as Chad slowly dragged her body back up onto the ledge. She felt sorry for what she had tried to do to her, and deeply regretted that there was no way to warn Sharon if she didn't make it.

Or was there a way?

"You're almost up," Chad said.

CHAPTER
ELEVEN

"DIDN'T THERE USED TO BE A BRIDGE HERE?" SHARON asked.

"Yes," Chad said.

"What happened to it?"

"It was old," Chad said. "I think it fell down."

Two days had passed since the end of the trial. The afternoon was bright and warm; there wasn't a cloud in the sky. Sharon and Chad had hiked into Sunset National Park from the direction of the lake this time. Chad had been right about the difficulty of the terrain; without his assistance, she doubted she would have made it this far. Sharon could well understand why Chad had brought the group in from the west the last time they had hiked to the cliff. But she had insisted they take the eastern entrance when she learned they could get to the cliff in only two hours. She wanted plenty of time to look around.

The only trouble was, she didn't know what she was looking for.

They were on the south side of the river, on a ledge, staring a hundred feet down into the foaming rapids.

"Is there another bridge?" Sharon asked.

"No," Chad said.

"But how are we going to cross to the other side? I want to return to exactly where Ann jumped."

Chad pulled off his sunglasses and peered at her. "Can you keep a secret?" he asked.

"As long as I'm not hauled back into court and told to testify about it."

"I know another way across this river."

"Where is it?"

Chad gestured to the river below. "We have to go down there and hike back downstream. It's not far."

"We couldn't have taken this way coming in?" she asked.

"No. Not without rock-climbing equipment."

"What are we going to do? Swing across the water on a vine?"

He chuckled. He had lost the gloominess of the trial. "You'll see."

The way down to the water was steep, but Sharon couldn't complain. Simply walking in the open air was a pleasure after her long confinement. If only the purpose of her visit was less serious. She was grateful she had Chad to talk to. She hoped she had not leaned on him too hard to accompany her.

Quickly they reached the floor of the gorge and turned back in the direction of the lake, walking beside the edge of the river. The exercise had Sharon sweating, and she was glad for the fine spray as it settled lightly on her exposed skin, soothing in its delicious coolness.

"This is heaven," she said. She didn't even need the insect repellent Chad had given her. The mosquitoes were leaving her alone this time.

"It's a beautiful day," Chad agreed.

She shook her head. "We were having such a great time that weekend." She stopped. "I'm sorry."

"You can talk about it."

"You must be tired of listening to me."

"Never."

She smiled. "How did you ever get to be so nice?"

"I had to make up for my looks."

"Stop that. You're handsome. I think you are."

"Yeah," he said. "But you just got out of jail."

She laughed. "I am appreciating everything a lot more. Do you know what I had for lunch right after the trial?"

"Filet mignon."

"Pizza. Pepperoni with a thick crust. I dreamed about one the whole time I was in my cell. I drew pictures of pizzas on the wall." She groaned. "But it was the craziest meal. My lawyer kept putting his hand on my knee. Even with my mother sitting right there. She was encouraging him! She thinks he's the man for me. *She* told him to give me a call next week."

"That was John Richmond?"

"Yeah."

"He's a smart guy," Chad said.

"You ain't kidding. Can you believe him figuring out Ann and Paul's plan?"

"No. Have you seen Fred since you got out?"

"He spoke to me on the phone yesterday. He

apologized for the things he said after Ann went off the cliff. Then he said he had to go."

"Are you going out with him again?" Chad asked.

"No."

"Do you want to?"

"No. I discovered something about him I don't like. He's only nice when he has a few drinks in him." She poked him in the side. "Besides, I want to go out with you."

Chad brightened. "Really?"

"Yeah."

"Just as friends, though, right?"

She blushed. "Not necessarily."

"Did you take any hard drugs while you were in jail?"

"No! Why do you say that? Do I sound brain-damaged?"

"Well . . ." he said.

"Just because I want to go out with you?"

"Well . . ."

"Chad! You're a great guy." She lowered her voice. "Don't you want to go out with me?"

He hesitated. "Sure."

"You miss her, still, don't you?"

He stopped walking and looked at the cold water. The light seemed to fall from his face. "Especially in this place."

She touched his side. He had on a shirt, unlike when they had last hiked in these parts. "I shouldn't have dragged you here."

"It was my idea," he said.

"You know it wasn't."

He shrugged, embarrassed. "I'm flattered you're interested in me. It's just that—"

"I was never interested in you before?"

"I guess," he said reluctantly.

Sharon looked up at the clear sky. She had decided she should look up more often. Her sense of what was important needed expanding.

"Ever since I can remember," she said, "I've been thinking about my future. What I want to accomplish. How I'm going to get it. I would go to school and talk to everybody, and be nice and everything, but I was never really there. My mind was always on my music. No, my mind was on me. Just me. I was so self-centered, I never realized Jerry cared that much about me."

"You shouldn't dwell on it."

"But I want to. I want to think about others for a change. Jerry's not the only example." She was getting emotional. "Look at my best friend. Ann hated my guts, and I didn't even know it. What does that tell you?"

"Ann didn't hate you."

"She must have, to try what she did." Sharon grimaced. "If only we'd talked about it. If only she had told me how she felt."

"Ann was confused," Chad said. He kicked a rock on the ground into the water. "So is my brother."

"Have you spoken to him since we were in the room?"

"No. And I'm not going to."

"You honestly think he killed her?"

"Let's just say I know he took advantage of her."

Sharon sighed. "Only a few weeks ago we were walking along this river like one big happy family."

Chad squeezed her hand where she had touched him. "What you just said means a lot to me."

"I'm glad." Sharon forced a smile. "On our first date, we have to go for pizza. I haven't gotten rid of my craving."

He grinned. "I might put my hand on your knee."

She messed up his hair. "In that case, I'm *not* bringing my mother."

They continued with their hike. Fifteen minutes later they began to wind upward along a narrow path that carried them several hundred feet above the river. Sharon was sensitive to heights. Looking down made her dizzy. They were halfway to the top of the cliff when Chad stopped before the opening of a cave.

"We're not going in there?" she said.

Chad pulled a flashlight from his backpack. "Don't panic. I have fresh batteries."

"But I want to cross the river."

"Trust me," he said.

She glanced into the cave. It was pitch-black. "I trust you."

They went inside. The floor was damp, the ceiling low. Sharon did not like caves. They reminded her of lions and tigers and bears and jail cells. She asked Chad if they might accidentally bump into a bear, and he said anything was possible. From then on she clung to the back of his pack. She had the knife he had given her before tucked snugly in her belt in its leather case, but she wished she had a flashlight of her own.

The cave sloped downward, turning in a slow curve to the right, and the damp floor began to disappear beneath an inch of flowing water. If the ground had been less rough, she surely would have slipped and slid into the bowels of the earth. The water was seeping through the walls, the ceiling—rain pouring through solid rock. It took her a while to realize what they were doing.

"This cave goes under the river!" she said.

"Exactly."

She tightened her grip on his pack. "What if the ceiling caves in?"

"Then we'll drown."

"You should have told me you were taking me this way."

"You wouldn't have come." He patted her hand. "Relax. This cave has existed for thousands of years. It'll last a few more minutes."

The ground ceased its downward slope, suddenly leveling out or, rather, disappearing beneath a cold black stream. Chad halted at the edge of it. Unless her sense of direction was reversed, the current was flowing *opposite* the direction of the Whipping River. She asked Chad about it and he nodded.

"It doesn't flow into Winter Lake," he said, his voice echoing in the long eerie cavern. "But deeper into the earth."

"Is it supplied by the water leaking through from the river?"

"Partly. But I think the lake itself must supply a portion of the water. You know those bridge builders that disappeared when they fell in Whipping River?" He nodded toward the center of the subterranean stream. "They probably came this way after sinking to the bottom of the lake."

Sharon shivered. Even if they'd had a powerful searchlight, she doubted they would have been able to penetrate to the end of the tunnel. It seemed to go on forever—more like a hole in the empty depths of space than a cave to the center of the earth. There was a distinct otherworldliness to the place. She didn't like it.

"How deep is it?" she asked.

"You'll see."

"Chad! We're not crossing it."

"It's hot outside. You'll dry in a few minutes."

"Does anyone else know about this cave?"

"I don't think so."

She clasped his hand. "You didn't tell Paul, did you?"

He was slow in answering. "No."

I just didn't want to step on Ann's body, that's all.

It was a horrible thought. She wished she hadn't had it. She couldn't get rid of it. Chad seemed to read her mind. He had that knack.

"Do you want me to carry you piggyback?" he asked.

"No. I might make you slip."

Then the light might go out. Horrible thoughts.

Hand in hand they took the plunge. The smooth ground went down quickly; thirty feet into the stream and the water was up to her waist. It was not merely cold. It was like frozen death. It crawled up her thighs and over her butt and then she couldn't feel her thighs and butt. She swallowed thickly and tasted ice.

"Don't be afraid," Chad whispered.

"What?"

"I'm going to turn off the light for a moment."

No! No! No!

The ice in her throat made her gag. Chad flicked off the flashlight without a word of protest from her. A dark blanket settled over her face. It was thick, impenetrable—she felt as if she were smothering. Chad let go of her hand, and she would have screamed if she could have found her mouth. Then his hands brushed the sides of her arms. She jumped at his touch, for an instant imagining that it was someone other than Chad.

Someone like a lost bridge builder.

"Don't be afraid," he repeated.

"I don't like this," she managed to get out.

"Listen."

In the silence of the black she heard a faint roar and tiny splashes. It was the river. They were directly beneath it. Drops struck the top of her head and her arms. Chad tightened his hold on her arms.

"Isn't this romantic?" he asked.

She couldn't stop trembling. "I hate it."

"You're not mad at me, are you?"

"No. But let's go. Turn on the light."

"You're sure?"

"Turn on the light, Chad!"

She appeared to surprise him. He backed up a step. For a moment he didn't speak, didn't seem to breathe —she couldn't even tell he was there. Then his light came on in her eyes, and she winced in pain. He hastily turned it upward. All she could see were spots. He grabbed her hand.

"Let's go," he said.

The stream rose as high as her chest, but no farther. Very soon the water level began to fall—the river

appeared no wider than the river above. Stepping onto
the far shore, they were met with half a dozen caves.
Chad led her to the second one on the left. He had
partially explored the others, he said. Once he had
been lost beneath the ground for hours, long after his
flashlight had died. He began to tell her his bizarre
tale, but she stopped him. She could already sympa-
thize; that was as close as she wanted to get to the
event. She was amazed he hadn't gone insane wander-
ing around down here for so long. She squeezed his
hand tighter and begged him to hurry them to the
surface.

The cave rose quickly upward. It was more slippery
than the first, and she had trouble staying on her feet.
She was in too much of a hurry. At the first glimpse of
light she let go of his hand and dashed for the exit. He
thought that was funny. Giggling like a little kid, he
quickly caught her and passed her by.

"Chad!" she complained.

He didn't slow down, and she might have lost her
trust in him if a moment later an abrupt turn in the
cave hadn't dramatically increased the level of indi-
rect sunlight. Sharon giggled along with him, as much
out of relief as anything else. Chad had just been
playing with her. They were close to the surface.

The exit let out at a lower elevation than the
entrance, far closer to the surface of the river. Chad
pointed out the ledge on the other side, where they
had been standing less than an hour before. He told
her to relax and dry off for a few minutes while he
went hunting for lunch. He was in a silly mood. She
wondered if he had meant to kiss her while they stood
beneath the river. Even in the warm sunlight, her

gooseflesh remained. Chad had a thing or two to learn about timing.

Chad left Sharon alone. He said he would search the area for signs of anything suspicious, whatever that meant. She hadn't explained to him why she wanted to come back. Intuition was not something that could be explained.

Sharon decided she'd use the time alone for a short break. Throwing off her backpack and stripping down to her underwear, she stretched out on a flat boulder beside a small pool that had collected in a calm circle off the main river—a mellow offspring of the frantic rapids. She started out shivering, but the heat of the sun's rays soon penetrated deep into her skin. She began to dry off, to relax and doze. However, she didn't want to sleep. That would be leaving herself too open for another of Chad's pranks. Besides, she only had her underwear on. She rolled over on her side and cupped her palm and dipped it into the gentle pool. She was thirsty, and the clear water looked inviting.

Sharon tasted only a sip of the water before she spat it out.

Clear water. Clear as glass.

The pool was four feet deep. She could see the bottom. Everything on the bottom.

"What's your name? I'm Ann Rice. You're Sharon McKay, right?"

Hello. Goodbye. Goodbye, Ann.

The pants were tattered, the shirt and jacket torn. A coil of rope, perhaps as long as five hundred feet and entwined with heavy moss-covered stones, circled the lower body. No one in the school had approached Ann's incredible beauty, and even in that horrible moment of discovery, Sharon felt sad that she would never again be able to remember Ann as she had been. Sharon looked for only a fraction of a second before she clenched her eyes shut, but the horrible image burned too deep. The swollen black cheeks. The twisted purple mouth. The pink slit throat. It was a pity, Sharon thought, that Ann could no longer close her own eyes and look away from what was left of her body. But the fish in the river must have been hungry.

Ann's eyes were missing.

Sharon turned away and vomited.

CHAPTER TWELVE

THE COP WAS THE SAME GUY WHO HAD ARRESTED SHARON weeks before—the obese and abrasive Lieutenant George Artso. He was full of suspicious questions. It was obvious that what he really wanted to do was snap the cuffs on her and whisk her away in the helicopter to another cramped cell. It was amazing the helicopter even flew with his fat ass sitting in it.

After discovering the body Sharon and Chad had immediately gone in search of help. Fortunately, they had not gone far when they stumbled across a park ranger who had a CB. Less than two hours had elapsed since Sharon had gagged on her sip of water. There wasn't a thing left in her stomach. She had thrown up for the fourth time ten minutes before. Lieutenant George Artso had stood and watched. He thought she was a great little actress.

"I don't get this," Artso was saying, a tiny white notepad in his fat hands, a half-smoked cigar hanging out the corner of his mouth beneath a greasy mustache. "You just *happened* upon the body. How did you do that?"

"We told you," Chad said. "By chance."

"I'm asking the young lady here," Artso said.

"Her name's Sharon," Chad said, insulted.

"By chance," Sharon said.

"What did you two do?" Artso asked. "Agree to say the same thing?"

"Why do you assume we're lying to you?" Chad asked.

Artso put away his notepad and poked Chad in the chest with his finger. "I'll tell you why, boy. My men and I searched this river for two weeks solid and didn't see a sign of this body. We must have walked by this spot a half dozen times. Then you two are out for a nature walk and you stumble right on it."

"Did you examine the bottom of this pool when you conducted your search?" Chad asked. "The body was weighted with stones. It was purposely sunk. If Sharon hadn't just happened to lie down beside the pool, Ann's body might not have been discovered for years."

"That's what I don't like here," Artso snarled. "This *just-happened* crap. Where were you exactly when the young lady found the body?"

Chad pointed to a ridge above the pool. "Over there."

"What were you doing?"

"Taking a piss," Chad said.

"So you didn't see where the body was to begin with?"

"That sounds like an incriminating question," Chad said.

"If you're going to arrest me, do it and get it over with," Sharon said. "I'm getting sick of listening to this."

Artso snorted. "You can get sick at the drop of a hat, can't you?"

"She was my friend!" Sharon yelled at him, gesturing to the white blanket that lay below them, on the rocks beside the pool. The two police officers standing near the body glanced up at the noise. "I've known her for years. We did everything together." She poked Artso in the chest with her finger. "You're a jerk. I remember that night a month ago. You made me hike five miles with my hands cuffed behind my back, and I hadn't done anything wrong!"

Artso pushed away her finger. "You've got a temper, bitch. I saw it that night I arrested you. That's why I cuffed you the way I did. I don't care what that fool court decided. So your hotshot lawyer got you off. In my book you're still guilty." He noticed a glint of metal in her hand. "What's that?"

Sharon drew back her hand. "Nothing."

"What is it?" Artso insisted.

"A ring," Chad said.

The ring belonged to Ann. Sharon had given it to Ann on her birthday two years before. It was nothing fancy—a one-tenth-carat ruby surrounded by a few diamond chips. It had cost Sharon a hundred and twenty bucks—every cent she had at the time. Sharon always took pride in the fact that Ann wore it day in and day out when she owned jewelry that cost a hundred times as much. Ann obviously valued the sacrifice, and their friendship.

The ring had an amusing story connected with it. When Sharon had thought of the idea for the present, she had approached Chad and asked what Ann's birthstone was. Chad knew about stuff like that. He said ruby, and he sounded confident. But he was wrong, or maybe he had misunderstood the question. *His* birthstone was a ruby—his birthday was July twelfth. Ann's birthday was June twelfth—hers was pearl. When Sharon gave Ann the present, the mistake naturally came to light. Sharon was embarrassed and wanted to exchange the ring. But Ann wouldn't hear of it. She said the red ruby went well with her dark hair. And, of course, it did—everything went well with Ann's beautiful hair. From then on, in private, they always jokingly referred to the ring as "Chad's ring." They never told him about his mistake. He was sensitive to things like that. He would have died.

In retrospect, however, Sharon didn't understand why Ann hadn't destroyed the ring the day Jerry died.

Sharon had found the ring not far from where she discovered the body, on the north ledge where the missing bridge had been tied. While waiting for the police helicopter to arrive, Sharon had tried to distract herself by studying the ledge. She was surprised to see that the bridge ropes had been severed with a knife. Sharon considered this important because if Ann had planned on reaching her getaway car, she would have to cross the bridge. Sharon thought it highly unlikely that Ann knew about Chad's cave. The clue raised the possibility that Paul had severed the bridge ropes before their weekend began, in order to stop Ann at this spot so he could kill her and bury her in the pond. Sharon had been meaning to discuss the theory with Chad.

Sharon didn't know why Ann had finally chosen to remove the ring. It seemed unlikely the ring could have fallen off in her struggle with Paul. Nevertheless, Sharon was happy she had found it. The ring brought back warm memories. She certainly didn't want to give it up to a sadistic bastard who would undoubtedly try to use it against her in a court of law.

"Let me see it," Artso said.

"No," Sharon said.

"Where did you get it?" Artso demanded.

Chad sighed. "It belonged to Ann."

"You snitched it off her finger?" Artso asked, amazed. "That's sick."

"You're sick," Sharon said coldly.

Artso stuck out his fat palm. "Hand it over. That's state evidence."

Chad touched her shoulder. "You better give it to him, Sharon. We'll get it back later."

A tear ran over Sharon's cheek. She held out the ring. "That's the present I gave to Ann on her sixteenth birthday. I didn't *snitch* it off her finger. You shouldn't say that."

"Sure you didn't," Artso said, pocketing the ring. "And those are real tears you're crying." He turned to Chad. "I'd mind myself, boy, if I was planning on spending the night in this park with this bitch. She's got a record when she's alone with people that would make me mighty uneasy."

Chad acted bored. "Can we go?"

Artso had nothing to hold them on. He left in the helicopter with the other two officers and the body. Another tear rolled over Sharon's cheek. She raised her hand and waved as the helicopter flew out of sight.

"Goodbye, Ann," she said.

Chad wanted to call it a day. He suggested they hike back to the car and drive home. A small orange towel had been found tied to Ann's head. It was from a sleazy hotel in San Diego. The evidence was pointing more and more to Paul as the murderer. The discovery of Ann's body seemed to sap Chad's strength. Sharon felt guilty for insisting they continue their investigation and return to the cliff where they had camped. She was being selfish, but she wanted to see with her own eyes the hole in the side of the cliff that had held the metal hook and Ann's rope. She realized she must still be trying to prove to herself that John was right about what had happened that night. Chad gave in reluctantly.

"It'll be close to dark by the time we get there," he said. "We'll have to spend the night."

"I don't mind," Sharon said.

CHAPTER THIRTEEN

*T*HEY REACHED THE TOP OF THE CLIFF HALF AN HOUR before the sun set. Sharon was exhausted by then. Pacing a cell for the last month had not kept up her endurance. Chad, in fact, had to take her backpack the last mile—it was very steep, and she was panting.

The view from the top was even more breathtaking this time. In the glow from the orange evening sun, the entire gorge was ablaze. Unlike last time, the air was perfectly still. A deep peace seemed to permeate the area. But Sharon now knew how deceptive appearances could be. The river sounded miles away, but it was still only five hundred feet straight down.

Chad forbade her to go over the side of the cliff and search for the hole created by the rock hook. He said such an attempt was dangerous under normal circumstances for someone as inexperienced as she was, and that the fading light would make it doubly so. They argued for several minutes before reaching a compromise. He'd go over the side and find the hole so that she'd be able to sleep that night, but they'd leave the rope in place. In the morning she'd get a chance. She had listened to so much talk the past few weeks, she wanted proof she could see and touch.

Wasn't Ann's slit throat enough for me?

Chad secured his line to the same stone Paul had used. He was confident in his skills; he didn't want Sharon to feed him the rope as he had done for Paul. Because there was no wind, and some light remained, it was safe for Sharon to stand at the edge and follow Chad's descent. Actually, she *knelt* at the edge. Looking five hundred feet straight down from a standing position made her uneasy. It was impossible to imagine the guts Ann had possessed to make such a leap.

"Careful," she told Chad as he eased himself down. He had the rope wrapped twice around his waist, through a special belt equipped with a series of stainless steel hooks. He sprang nimbly from crack to crack, like a cat.

"That's sound advice for any rock climber," he said.

"How did you get started in this sport?"

"I'm crazy."

"Do you have to go down so fast?" she asked, worried for him.

"This isn't fast. I remember Paul spent most of his time fifty feet down. That's probably where the pin was. There's a slight ledge there."

"I think I see it." A strip of rock about a yard long jutted out less than a foot from the side. "How could anyone have stood on that?"

"They'd have to be crazy," Chad said.

He reached the ledge as the last rays of the sun peeled off the base of the cliff, the shadow cast by the far side of the gorge rising steadily toward them like a dark hand reaching up from beneath the earth. The sun would set soon. Sharon couldn't stop thinking about the black stream that secretly ran under Whipping River. Its existence struck her as symbolic of her own situation. The cold and dark Ann Rice existing beneath the warm and bright one?

No. Something else. What?

"Be careful," she said.

Chad shifted gingerly on the ledge. "You said that already."

"Do you see it?"

"I'm looking."

"You're about to lose the sun," she said.

"I know." Chad swept the stone wall with the palm of his hand as well as his eyes. "I see it."

"It's there? You're sure?"

"Yes."

Sharon drew in a deep shuddering breath. "Then it's true."

"Oh, I think it's true," Chad said.

"You really think Paul slit Ann's throat?"

"He must have."

"But could this hole be from someone else's pin?"

"That's possible," he said. "I want to come up now."

"Can I help you?"

"I can do it."

Chad pulled himself back up with little difficulty. He had amazingly powerful arms for someone so thin.

He did consent to take her hand as he stepped onto the ledge. She had a brief moment of panic before he righted himself when she felt as if she was about to be pulled over the edge. She should listen to him and stay out of his way. She began to have second thoughts about looking at the hole tomorrow. There seemed no point to it.

They should have immediately set about preparing camp, but they ended up sitting near the edge of the cliff and watching the sun go down. The day had given them both much to absorb, too much. Chad had a brother who was about to stand trial for first-degree murder. She had a memory of the rotting body of a friend who would have murdered her if she'd had the chance. But was that true? Ann could have pushed her off the cliff if she'd wanted. She'd had plenty of opportunities. Sharon asked Chad what he thought.

"Don't ask me to figure Ann out," he said. "I can't figure myself out."

"Do you know what her last words to me were? I asked her what she was going to do with her life. She told me she couldn't think of anything. Isn't that sad?"

"She might have been setting up her phony suicide/murder."

"Maybe," Sharon said. "But there was something in her voice. I think she was trying to tell me how empty her life was. If only I'd stopped to listen to her."

"If her life was empty, it was because she was unwilling to share it with anyone."

"Except Paul."

Chad picked up a stone and tossed it over the side. His sharp tone surprised her. "He doesn't count."

"You don't want to talk about it," she said. "I'm sorry."

He shrugged. "It's not as though I grew up with him. I don't care about him."

"You're not serious?"

"I am." He looked at her and smiled. "But I care about you."

"And I care about you, Chad."

He put his arm over her shoulder. "It might be cold tonight."

She laughed uneasily. "I thought you said the conditions were supposed to be mild?"

"Did I say that?"

She hugged her knees to her chest. "I remember."

He leaned closer. She could feel his warm breath on her cheek. "It's late," he said. "I don't know if we'll be able to find wood for a fire."

She was grateful for the poor light. She knew she must be blushing. "Thank God we have *two* warm sleeping bags to curl up in."

"Sharon?"

"What?"

"May I kiss you?"

She hesitated. No guy had ever asked before—most just did it. "Sure."

He kissed her briefly. Then he put his other arm around her and started to kiss her again. She turned her head away.

"What's the matter?" he asked quickly.

"Nothing."

"What?"

She didn't know what was wrong. But the moment his lips had touched her mouth, she felt suddenly sick to her stomach. It probably had to do with Ann's body; she still couldn't get the sight of it out of her mind. She knew she never would. But her fit of nausea passed quickly.

"I'm sort of a slow kind of girl," she said gently.

He released her. "I shouldn't have done that."

"Why not?"

"I'm no good with girls," he said.

"That's not true. Any girl would feel lucky to be here with you."

"Really?"

She nodded. "This girl does."

He thought about that a moment. "Can I tell you something?"

"Of course," she said.

"I never kissed a girl before."

"Boy. What an insult! You just kissed me!"

He looked confused. Then he grinned. He must be getting used to her sense of humor. "How was I?"

She patted his hand. "Excellent."

He took her hand in his. "But I shouldn't be bothering you. You've had a trying day. I wanted to sock that cop in the mouth, the way he kept after you."

"I'm glad you didn't. He would have shot you." Sharon looked at the western sky. It was a glorious shade of red. It reminded her of Ann's ruby.

Why did she pull off the ring just before she died?

The question had plagued Sharon since she'd found the ring on the ledge. And that was another thing that bothered her. Chad had been wrong about the bridge. Lieutenant Artso said it had been in place until a month ago.

"Chad," she said. "Remember what Artso said about us happening across Ann's body? What did you think of that?"

"Nothing. Artso's just an asshole."

"But isn't it strange that no one else saw the body after all this time?"

"I doubt Artso and his men spent half a day looking for it."

"You really think so? I don't know."

He peered at her curiously. The light was going fast. His face was dark, particularly his eyes. "What don't you know, Sharon?"

"I was just thinking, is all."

"What?" he asked.

"Nothing."

"You said that after I kissed you. What does that mean?"

Sharon frowned. Chad's tone had changed. He sounded like he did when he spoke of Paul, or Ann, for that matter. And he had always used to speak of Ann with such love. Bitterness in him seemed so out of place. She took her hand back from him.

"When I say nothing, I mean nothing," she replied. "I was just commenting on what an incredible coincidence it was that I should be the one to find Ann. It's no wonder Artso was suspicious."

"Suspicious?"

"Yeah. Couldn't you tell by the way he was acting?"

"He was suspicious of you," Chad said.

"That's what I'm saying. How could he be suspicious of you? You weren't even there."

"That's right."

"Yeah," she said.

An uncomfortable silence followed. He suddenly stood. "I'm going to look for wood."

She stared up at him, wondering what was wrong. "OK."

"I won't be gone long."

"Fine," she said.

He pointed to where the sun had set. "The sky's a beautiful red."

"It's gorgeous."

"It reminds me of the ruby you gave Ann on her birthday." He turned to go. "You have to be sure to get that ring back."

She stopped him, grabbing his leg. "I was just thinking that."

"What?"

"About the sunset and Ann's ruby. I was thinking exactly the same thought."

Chad grinned. "I must be able to read your mind."

Sharon let go of his leg, feeling something terribly wrong and unable to pinpoint what it was. Yet this feeling—she knew that the reason for it would come to her momentarily, and that it would make her sick to her stomach again. Like when she had found Ann's bloated body.

Like when I kissed Chad.

Those two events—they had nothing in common. One had been horrible beyond description. The other had been pleasurable.

"What's the matter?" Chad asked.

It should have been pleasurable.

"Nothing," she muttered.

"You're sure?"

"Yes."

"Do you feel all right?"

She stared at the sky. Such a deep red. Like blood. "No."

"What's wrong?" he repeated.

"I'm cold."

Like when we walked across your black river. You tried to kiss me then, but you didn't. I told you I hated the place, Chad. I was afraid of the dark. Even though there was nothing there except us.

Sharon suddenly felt afraid, even before the source of her fear came into complete focus. For already she could see the hole in the center of it, the red glittering on the top of it. The police said Ann had a nasty cut on the top of her head. She might have cracked her skull when she went over the cliff, they said. One cop was amazed she hadn't bled to death from the cut. Of course, Ann had bled to death from another kind of cut. Someone had slit her throat. But Ann was no one to have been taken by surprise. She must have seen that someone coming. Someone she recognized.

Because Ann had removed the ring on purpose.

"I'll build you a fire," Chad said.

A ring Ann had received long before Paul had come into her life. Two years ago, on her birthday.

Sharon realized the answer had been right in the palm of her hand! Ann had left the ring on the ledge to warn her!

Chad's ring!

"You do that," Sharon whispered.

Chad turned and walked away from the ledge. Sharon watched him go with burning eyes and shattering new insight. Slowly the shadows enfolded him as he moved away. They fit him well, naturally, and it was no wonder he had been able to survive for hours with his mind unaffected when his flashlight had failed in the darkness deep beneath the ground. It was because his mind was already cracked, already filled with darkness.

It had been no coincidence she had found the body. Chad had led her directly to it. After first showing her where he had kept it hidden all the time the others searched the river.

At the limit of Sharon's vision, Chad stopped.

Oh, no. Oh, God.

Her tone must have alerted him, her comment on the coincidence.

He knew she knew!

He turned slowly. Watching her as she watched him. It was as if their minds had synchronized. He was waiting for her to make a move. Her eyes darted to her backpack. It sat twenty feet off to her left. Inside it was the knife Chad had given her. She had removed it from her belt earlier when it had begun to annoy her by banging against her leg. Her backpack was tied shut. It would take several seconds to open. She had slipped the knife down the side of the pack, near the bottom. It would take several seconds to dig it out.

Call to him. Say anything. Tell him to get you a nice fat log.

Sharon couldn't speak, and had she been able to, she knew her dry throat would have alerted him as well if she had shouted out the word *murderer*.

He took a step in her direction. Stopped.

Raise your arm. Wave. Blow him a kiss. Anything!

"Sharon?" he called.

She raised her arm and shook it feebly.

Chad took another step toward her. Paused. Then another.

Sharon crouched to her feet.

"Sharon?" he called, and he began to quicken his stride.

The pressure was unbearable. Sharon leapt. Straight for her backpack. As she did so, Chad broke into a sprint. Straight for her backpack.

Sharon got to it first—she was a lot closer. The cord that secured the top flap was tied in the same simple bow every kid in the country used to tie their tennis shoes. Grabbing both loose strings and pulling them in opposite directions, the bow immediately knotted. She couldn't believe it. She began to panic and tried breaking the string. Fat chance—she only succeeded in burning two lines across the back of her fingers. She looked up. Chad had already made up half the distance to her!

Stop pulling on it. A child can undo this type of knot.

Sharon concentrated on the structure of the knot. Her difficulty soon became apparent. The end of one string had caught in the bow. All she had to do was pull that end free and the knot would . . .

The knot opened. Quickly Sharon threw back the flap and dug into the sack. Her fingers encountered a pair of underwear, a T-shirt, more underwear. Why had she brought so much underwear? She should have brought a goddamn gun! Where was that knife? Could Chad have removed it? No, impossible—the pack hadn't been out of her sight for a moment.

He's almost on top of me!

Sharon's hand brushed what might or might not have been the tip of the leather knife case when the pressure finally got to her again. With Chad twenty feet away and bearing down at incredible speed, she dropped the backpack and jumped to her feet, quickly backing away. Chad halted his mad dash and placed himself between her and the pack. He began to circle her warily, boxing her in against the ledge.

"What are you doing?" he asked.

"Nothing."

"What are you doing?" he demanded.

"Nothing!" she cried.

"You're up to something."

"I don't know what you're talking about."

He stopped. "You know, Sharon."

She stopped. "I don't know anything."

He took a step closer. He held out his hand. "Come here."

"No."

"Don't be afraid."

"I just want to leave, Chad. That's all I want."

"That's not possible."

Tears stung her eyes. "Why not?"

He shook his head sadly. "Let's not fool ourselves. You figured it out. You know it was me. I can't let you go."

"I won't tell anybody."

"Yes. You'll tell." He took another step closer. "I'm sorry."

She backed up farther. "What are you going to do?"

"What I have to do."

She glanced over her shoulder. Ten more feet and

she would walk off the edge. That's what he wanted. "You're going to kill me."

"I don't want to, Sharon."

"Then stop," she wept, holding up her hands, begging. "For the love of God, just stop. I'm your friend, Chad. Please don't do this to me."

He stopped. For the moment. Deep distress creased his features. "How did you know?"

"Ann's ring. It's a ruby. It's your birthstone. You made a mistake when you told me to buy a ruby. Ann and I used to call it Chad's ring."

His face crumpled. "Her birthday wasn't the same day as mine?"

"No. It was a month earlier."

"She left it for you to find."

"Yes."

"She wanted to warn you."

"Let me go, Chad. I've never hurt you."

Chad clenched his fists. "She hated me."

"No."

He pressed his hands to his eyes. "How do you know? You didn't even know how she felt about you."

Sharon began to edge away from the cliff. "We can talk about it, Chad."

"There's nothing to talk about. I did the right thing. She used to sleep with Paul. I could hear them in the bedroom when I was mowing the lawn. My girl having scx with my own brother!"

"I don't know anything about that."

Chad pulled his hands away from his eyes. "Where are you going?"

She froze. "Nowhere."

"You're as bad as her!"

"No."

"You wouldn't even kiss me!"

"I kissed you a few minutes ago. I was the first girl ever to kiss you. Don't you remember?"

He nodded to himself, appearing to calm down. She had never seen mood swings like this in him before.

Of course, she had never seen him murder someone, either.

"I didn't mean to yell at you," he said.

"It's all right."

He shrugged helplessly. "What can I do, Sharon?"

"Let me go."

"You'll tell everybody it was me."

"I swear to you in the name of Almighty God I won't."

"You're lying. I'll be put in jail. Paul will go free, unpunished. It's not fair. I can't let it happen."

Sharon stared at him. "Can you kill me?"

He stared back. "Yes. I have no choice."

Sharon believed him. She also believed further conversation was not going to improve her situation. She came to a decision, unquestionably the most important decision she had ever made. She made a dash for it. Chad moved to block her way. But he had mistaken her intentions. She was not aiming for the trail that led down from the cliff.

Sharon was going over the cliff. Her way.

Grabbing the rope and pulling it tight, she balanced the soles of her shoes on the sharp edge for a moment. A look of comprehension filled Chad's face. He leapt toward her just as she jumped off the side.

"Do you have to go down so fast?"

Sharon put Chad to shame with her speed. It took her only a couple of heartbeats to reach the tiny ledge. It was an experience her senses barely registered, just a quick sliding motion, but it cost her a fair portion of the flesh on both her palms. She was lucky that was all it cost her. She had never practiced sudden braking at high altitudes before.

Yeah, I'm one lucky girl.

Sharon tilted her head back; the sting in her palms was incredible. Chad stared down at her from fifty feet above, looking a hundred feet tall in the lengthening shadows. He kicked the rope with his foot, trying to upset her balance. Letting out a gasp, Sharon released the rope and pressed her back to the stone wall. She spread out her arms and tried not to look down. Sandy gravel crunched under her shoes. The ledge was slippery as well as cramped.

"That was foolish," Chad said.

"I don't know. I'm still alive."

"I'm going to have to come down and get you."

"Why don't you just throw some rocks at me?"

"There aren't many loose rocks around here." He crouched by the side. "Do you have any questions?"

"Yeah. Where do you find a good parachute around here?"

"You're a brave girl, Sharon. So was Ann."

"I hope she gave you a good fight."

He nodded solemnly. "She came within a hair of killing me."

"How could you do it, Chad?"

"It gets a lot easier the third time around."

Sharon's stomach turned. She had never thrown up into a whole gorge before. She came close to another first. "What did you do?"

"I smothered Ann's mother. I was the one who shot Jerry."

"Why?" she cried.

"They didn't like me."

"Jerry was your best friend!"

"That's what I thought. But he was going to betray me. It's a long story."

"How did you convince Ann to jump off this cliff?"

"I let her think it was her idea." He paused. "I don't suppose that's going to work with you."

I can't just stand here and wait for this guy to come to me!

Sharon's fear tightened her guts into an agonizing ball. She trembled as Ann's empty eyes flashed before her eyes. Her vision blurred with salty tears and she had to close her eyes. Chad would throw her in the same river with the same fish!

"It would make it a lot easier if you would just jump," he said.

She shook her head, moaning to herself.

"I'm tired, Sharon."

Damn him! Damn him!

It was such an arrogant comment on his part, it pissed her off, and that was the best thing that could have happened to her. A rush of anger shot through her that was almost as good as a goddamn gun. She stopped trembling. Her fear receded. There was no time for it. She swore to herself she would put up a better fight than Ann.

Chad's going to feed the fish tonight.

Wiping her eyes, Sharon searched the immediate area for a loose stone, a branch, anything she could use as a weapon. There was nothing. She checked her pockets. What she found at first seemed as good as nothing: an aerosol can of insect repellent and a tiny jar of petroleum jelly.

"You won't be able to convince a soul I committed suicide," she called, stalling for time. Insect repellent in the eyes was no fun. Petroleum jelly was lousy on the grip. Sharon put two and two together and came up with an interesting idea.

"I won't have any trouble," Chad said. "The police saw how upset you were at finding Ann's body. I'll just tell them you freaked out and jumped."

She held out one of her hands. "How will you explain these rope burns?"

"Let me worry about that, Sharon."

"Just trying to be helpful." She popped open the jar of jelly and scooped some onto her fingers. She began to rub it on the length of rope in front of her. Chad paid her scant attention. He was watching the sky again. The ruby red was fading to charcoal black. And she had used to tell people what a gem he was. "Did you plant the rock hook for Fred to find?" she called.

"Yes. I knew someone would find it."

"Did you give John the book that got him thinking?"

"I practically handed it to him."

"Did you cut the bridge down?"

"Ann did," he said.

"Why?"

"She thought I was on the other side."

Sharon continued to work with the jelly. "Tell me about your childhood?"

"What do you want to know?"

"Oh, the usual. Did anyone try to smother you or cut your throat?"

He was insulted. "You seem to think this is a joke."

"Do you hear me laughing?"

He stood. "We should get this over with."

"Don't let me hurry you."

Chad didn't answer. He picked up the rope and, momentarily turning his back to her, began to lower himself over the side, not bothering to thread the rope through the steel hooks in his special rock-climbing belt. He must have thought she was going to be easy. Sharon took advantage of the opportunity to finish smearing the entire rope—from over her head to the bottom of her feet—with the Vaseline. Stuffing the jar back in her pocket, she pulled the cap off the aerosol can and held her index finger poised above the plunger, clutching it in her right hand, out of sight at the side of her body.

"Hang on," Chad called. "I'm almost there."

"You just take your sweet time," she whispered.

Chad came down slowly. She wasn't sure what he had planned, but she imagined kicking her in the face would be a good place for him to start. His actions reinforced her suspicion. He stopped his descent a body length short of the ledge, with his feet just above her head. He had superb coordination. He balanced on the side of the cliff as if he were sitting on a stone wall.

His hands were a good three feet above where her petroleum jelly began. She had to get his grip lower, his face closer.

"Hi," she said.

"You can make this easier on the two of us if you'll just jump."

"All right. On one condition."

"What?"

She removed her gold necklace with her left hand. Ann had given it to her two Christmases ago. It contained a flawless two-carat emerald—her birthstone. "You have to give this to my mom."

He shook his head. "That will look too suspicious."

"I don't want the stone to crack in the fall. You know how soft emeralds are. Look, you'll be the first one to reach my body. Put it back around my neck when I'm dead, but take it for now. Please?"

He considered. "Then you'll jump?"

"I promise."

"This isn't a trick?"

"Chad! The necklace isn't going to explode in your hand."

He nodded. "You've got a deal." He eased himself down a couple of feet, reached out with his left hand. "Give it to me."

"My pleasure."

In a single swift motion, Sharon dropped the necklace and raised the insect repellent and sprayed it directly in his eyes. She got off a perfect shot from less than a foot away. Chad lost his grip on the rope. He fell.

No, he slipped. There was a big difference. The sting

to his eyes caused him to drop into her petroleum jelly zone. Once there, he slipped all the way to the end of it before regaining his grip. Again his athletic prowess amazed her. Anybody else would have been flying through the air by now.

His head was now level with the ledge. With her feet.

"Sharon!" he complained.

She kicked him in the face as hard as she could. "You bastard!"

The force of her kick sent him careening away from the side. He let out a loud cry. Unfortunately, his grip remained firm. As he swung back toward her, he tried to grab her shin. She was too fast for him. Moving to the side, she kicked him again and again, in the mouth, the eyes, the nose. In seconds his face was a mass of blood. Yet he continued to hang on, all the while shouting at her.

"Stop it!" he cried. "Don't! You're hurting me!"

Sharon began to despair of ever getting him to let go. With each kick she let fly, she risked losing her balance. One miss was all it would take to send her falling toward the river. Holding out the bug spray once more, she risked bending over and giving him another shot in the eyes.

That was a mistake. He grabbed the hand that held the can.

"Why are you doing this?" he demanded, his features a pulpy mess.

"Because you're a lousy kisser!"

"Don't say that!"

"Let go of me!"

"Quit kicking me!"

Sharon poked him in the eyes with her left hand. She had long nails—her piano teacher was always trying to get her to cut them. Once more her aim was perfect. The soft tissue made a sick squashing sound. Chad screamed and lost his grip.

For a fraction of a second. He regained it for what seemed the twentieth time at the very end of the rope, fifty feet below her. Would this guy never die? He raised his swollen face and tried to glare at her.

"You hurt my eyes!" he said.

"Well, excuse me!"

"Ann hurt my eyes!"

"Good for her!"

"I'm going to get you!"

Oh, God, he was climbing back up. Sharon leapt onto the rope, as high as she could, just above her stretch of petroleum jelly. She had only half the distance to climb, but surely, she thought, she must have less than half his strength. But pressing her feet against the rock wall, leaning back, and yanking upward, she was met with two surprises. Her fear had given her unnatural strength. Her grip was far stronger than she could have hoped. Also, even though the cliff looked relatively smooth, it was really pocked with numerous small holes and bumps that her feet quickly found. Sharon scurried up the cliff with the ease of a spider going up a bedroom wall. Dragging herself onto the top of the cliff, she turned and looked down.

Chad was already past the ledge!

"You're the lousy kisser!" he swore, coming toward her in huge leaps and bounds.

The knife!

Sharon dashed to the backpack. She dug her hand through the open flap. The thing that had felt like the knife case the first time had been the knife case. Pulling the blade free, she raced back to the ledge. The rope stretched taut above the ground between the rock and the edge. Sharon didn't bother to recheck Chad's position—it was irrelevant. She knelt and began to hack at the rope. The knife was blunt. She should have listened to Chad; he'd told her to sharpen it when he had given it to her. The individual rope strands plucked free at a maddeningly slow pace. On the other hand, the rope was thin. She didn't hack long before it snapped.

Thank God!

But there was no scream. Why didn't he scream?

Sharon crept to the edge. She had seen many thrillers in her day. She held the knife ready. If he was to reach up suddenly and grab her with a bloody claw, she was going to cut it off.

Sharon peeked over the edge.

"Looks like you won," Chad said, standing on the ledge, the severed rope in his hand.

Sharon clapped her hands with glee. "You're stuck!"

He nodded miserably. "I could feel you cutting the rope. I knew I wasn't going to make it to the top."

"You lost your nerve. You climbed back down. Coward!"

"Shut up."

She mocked him. "Don't worry. The police will help you up."

He wiped his bloody face with the back of his arm. "I'm not going to wait for the police."

Sharon stopped. "You're not going to try to climb up without a rope, are you?"

"If I do, what will you do?"

"Stab you. Cut off your fingers."

"I believe you." He scanned the rock that lay between them. It was now almost totally dark; she didn't know what he could see. "I would never make it the last ten feet, anyway. The cliff sticks out."

"Just stay there. I'll get someone to help you."

He shook his head. "You're not listening to me. I won't be here when you get back."

"Where are you going?"

"Down."

She didn't know why it upset her. He was a psychopath. He had caused pain to so many people. Until a minute ago she had been trying to kill him. But he had been her friend.

"You can't jump," she said.

"Why not?"

"Because I don't want you to."

"Why?"

"Because you're sick. You need help. You don't need to die."

"Am I sick?" he asked, his voice sad.

"Yes. But that doesn't mean you're not loved. I love you."

"You don't."

"I do. I let you kiss me. I wanted to go out with you."

"We can't still go out?"

Sharon sighed. "I'm afraid not, Chad."

"I'm going to jump."

"No!"

He wiped his face again. She had done a number on him. He was bleeding freely. He shifted on the ledge and looked down. "It's OK," he said. "I'm not afraid. I deserve it. I screwed up. Killing's a bad thing."

"Suicide is a bad thing. Please, listen to me. Give yourself time. Give yourself a few minutes. Think about what you're doing. This is a beautiful world. You belong here."

"No."

"Yes! I want you here!"

Chad paused. "Am I really a lousy kisser?"

Sharon dropped to her knees and reached her hand over the edge. The gesture was supposed to be a sign of support. But she realized then that it was useless. His insanity was like the stream beneath the ground. It only flowed in one direction, into deeper and deeper darkness. She was going to lose him.

"You were great, Chad. It was the best kiss I ever had."

"Honestly?"

"Yeah."

He nodded to himself. "That's something."

"Yeah."

"Would you mind if I scream?"

"Whatever you want, Chad."

He held out his hand in the same way she had. He smiled at her. "Before she died, Ann told me something you'll want to hear. She knew I was the one who killed Jerry. She said she was sorry for what she had tried to do to you. She said that she had made a mistake. That you were the best friend she ever had."

Sharon's eyes blurred with tears. "Thanks for telling me."

"No problem." He took a breath. "Goodbye, Sharon."

She closed her eyes. "Goodbye."

EPILOGUE

CHAD'S SCREAM ECHOED THROUGHOUT THE GORGE long after he hit the rocks below. It brought the police. Sharon was sitting alone by a fire of her own making when they set down on top of the cliff in their trusty helicopter. Lieutenant Artso had known where to find her. He wasted no time slapping on the handcuffs and reading her her rights. He found the severed rope, the knife with her prints on it. Naturally, he didn't believe her story. He treated her like dirt, although he seemed happy to have caught her in the act again. The charge against her was the same as before.

Murder in the first degree.

"Can't stop pushing your friends off these cliffs, can you, bitch?" Artso said as he crowded into the helicopter's back seat beside her. The pilot lifted into the air.

"I want to talk to my lawyer," she growled.

"You need a lawyer," Artso said, and he belched.
"I'll get off," she replied confidently.
John would get her off.
But his services might be expensive. . . .
"You get in trouble again and it's going to cost you."
Sharon wondered if she should get another lawyer.

Look for Christopher Pike's
See You Later

About the Author

CHRISTOPHER PIKE was born in Brooklyn, New York, but grew up in Los Angeles, where he lives to this day. Prior to becoming a writer, he worked in a factory, painted houses, and programmed computers. His hobbies include astronomy, meditating, running, playing with his nieces and nephews, and making sure his books are prominently displayed in local bookstores. He is the author of *Last Act, Spellbound, Gimme a Kiss, Remember Me, Scavenger Hunt, Final Friends* 1, 2, and 3, *Fall into Darkness, See You Later, Witch, Die Softly, Bury Me Deep, Whisper of Death, Chain Letter 2: The Ancient Evil, Master of Murder, Monster, Road to Nowhere, The Eternal Enemy, The Immortal, The Wicked Heart*, and *The Midnight Club, The Last Vampire*, and *Remember Me 2: The Return*, all available from Archway Paperbacks. *Slumber Party, Weekend, Chain Letter*, and *Sati*—an adult novel about a very unusual lady—are also by Mr. Pike.